# The Sense of an Elephant

*Marco Missiroli*

# The Sense of an Elephant

*Translated from the Italian by Stephen Twilley*

PICADOR

First published in the United Kingdom 2015 by Picador
an imprint of Pan Macmillan Ltd, a division of Macmillan Publishers Limited
Pan Macmillan, 20 New Wharf Road, London N1 9RR
Basingstoke and Oxford
Associated companies throughout the world
www.panmacmillan.com

ISBN 978-1-4472-4193-5



Originally published in Italy 2012 as *Il Senso dell'Elefante* by Ugo Guanda Editore, Parma



1 3 5 7 9 8 6 4 2

A CIP catalogue record for this book is available from the British Library.

Printed and bound by McPhersons Printing Group

*To Sauro Missiroli and Fiorella Vandi*

*Thank You*

If someone is to be born, that person will not be *blank*,
but a *moral* being, a subject of *value* – not of integration.

*Roland Barthes*

Only now is the child finally divested of all that he has been.

*Cormac McCarthy*

There was a man, things for this man were going so-so, the Flood came and he was on the roof of his house so he wouldn't drown, he asks God with all his faith to be saved and in his heart he knows that God will save him.

A boat comes, the man refuses it because he's certain that the Lord will come to save him, so he says No, thank you. Meanwhile the water is rising, another boat comes but he's waiting for God. Meanwhile the water has reached his throat, a third boat passes, No, thanks. So then he drowns.

When he arrives in Heaven and finally sees the Lord, he says to him, You promised to save me! God looks at him, says, Hold on now, I sent you three boats, what else do you want from me?

# 1

The concierge's lodge was a clean, orderly space, furnished with a fake wood table and two wicker chairs. Beside the lodge window were pigeonholes for the post and a shelf with a battered radio and a telephone. On another wall hung a pen-and-ink rendering of Milan Cathedral above an empty nail. The table's single drawer contained a square of cardboard with a suction cap and the message 'Back soon.' A folding door led behind to a tiny flat composed of a bedroom and a combined living area and kitchen. In addition to polishing every square inch of the floor, its previous occupant had left behind a packet of coffee and a virtually new stovetop percolator, a half-full bottle of olive oil and a bottle of body wash for sensitive skin. Also remaining were ten hooks in the bedroom wall, on each a copy of a set of keys to a flat above.

Pietro had not so much as touched the keys since becoming the new concierge a month earlier. He did so that afternoon, approaching one of the hooks and lifting off the keys to the Martini family's flat. Luca Martini, a doctor, and his wife, Viola, had gone to pick up their daughter from nursery school. He slipped the keys into a pocket and returned to the windowless bathroom to rinse out the cleaning cloth, then tossed it in a plastic bucket, poured in two capfuls of detergent and filled the bucket with water. Staggered with the weight as far as the entrance hall, where the stairs began. He wrung out the cloth, wiped down a step and scrambled up to the next, climbing backwards like a half-dismembered spider. He would wipe with one hand and support himself with the other, then lean on the cloth hand and pull the bucket up. Upon reaching the first floor he picked up the doormats of the three flats and continued immediately on to the second, where he stopped. Starting from the lawyer Poppi's door he lifted the doormat with 'Abandon all hope' in Gothic script, cleaned and moved on to the Martinis' mat. Rolled it aside and diligently wiped a grease stain from the marble. He stood. The door handle was covered with fingermarks. He used a handkerchief to remove them, returned it to his pocket and felt the metal scratch his palm. Pulled out the keys, inserted them in their respective keyholes and opened the door.

He entered with his eyes closed and took half a step further. Took another step and looked: out of the gloom appeared a hall stand with three dark overcoats and Sara's ladybird umbrella. The parquet squeaked. The entryway's single shelf held two framed photographs and a basket of old knick-knacks. One of the pictures was of Dr Martini as a little boy pretending to drive a parked Vespa. He looked straight over the handlebars, his mouth serious. The concierge picked up the picture, caressed the child's head and the hand gripping the accelerator. Brought the image closer, caressed it again, squeezed the frame till he trembled. Put it back and stared at the basket of knick-knacks. On top were an inkwell, a frog paperweight, a bicycle bell. He took the bell in his hand and wiped the top with a shirtsleeve. It was rusty and its lever worn. He turned it over. It didn't weigh much. He backed up with the bell in his palm and withdrew from the Martinis' flat.

'Pietro.'

He spun round.

'Mr Poppi.'

The concierge picked up the cloth and hid the bell inside it. Water dripped onto his shoes.

'I've nearly finished cleaning.'

'Inside and out, I see.' The lawyer abruptly doffed his hat. His shiny head shone. '*Kibitzer*, as the Jews say: busybody.' He swung his walking stick in a small arc, raised an eyebrow.

Pietro, his face reddening, lightly tossed the cloth back into the bucket.

'Accept my invitation, friend,' said the lawyer. 'Stop cleaning so thoroughly and come with me to the cafe on the corner – now. I'll treat you to a cappuccino you won't forget.'

'I still have two floors to do.'

'Trust me.' The lawyer opened his front door and stepped in, picked up a raincoat from the arm of a sofa and shook it out before putting it on. Pointed to the flat next to the Martinis'. 'Our Fernando is about to declare himself. To miss it would be a big mistake.'

The concierge indicated his bucket.

'It's your loss, kibitzer.' He turned on his heel and started down the stairs.

Pietro waited until the lawyer reached the entrance hall then went to the last door on the floor, behind which lived the strange boy Fernando. Lifted the mat, cleaned and returned downstairs without stopping. Slipped into the lodge and headed straight for the tiny flat, still in disarray since his arrival. He had bought a bed and placed it below the living area's small window. A projecting wall divided the area from the kitchenette, three wall cupboards and a table with a plastic flower-pattern tablecloth, a buzzing refrigerator. A row of plants stood in the only sliver of space here struck by natural light. Beside them he had piled bags of clothes and his bicycle, a nearly forty-year-old Bianchi with flat handlebars, which salty air had stripped of much of its paint.

He went into the bathroom and retrieved the rag from the bucket, unrolled it one edge at a time over the sink. Cradled the bell in his fist, dried it carefully as he went into the bedroom, a mostly empty chamber with a porthole window that looked out onto the courtyard. Hung up the Martinis' keys on their hook. Below the hooks, indistinct in the half-light, were a lamp and an open suitcase with boxes inside. Long and thin boxes, boxes with worn corners. From a cylinder-shaped box he drew out an envelope bearing a stamp dedicated to Emilio Salgari and containing a photograph and a letter on rice paper. Though he knew the contents of the letter by heart, he read it as if for the first time, and like the first time he did not breathe until he reached the end. The concierge put everything back, added the bell, and before leaving for the cafe gazed for a moment on his past.

The young priest saw her on a September morning that year as well, and that year as well the girl gazed up at his window as she rode by on her bicycle with the straw basket. She wore a sailor suit and rang her bell, *brring-brring*, not a bit embarrassed that it caused people in front of the church to turn round. From between the shutters he returned her gaze and closed his eyes. When he reopened them she was on the ground and the bicycle on top of her, screaming I killed it, I didn't see it, I killed the cat.

The young priest ran down into the street, slipped through the crowd around the girl. Went to her. She was holding her stomach but would not take her eyes off the cat.

'It's the priest's, it's dead,' someone said.

'The only ones who kill cats are witches and the scourges of God,' someone else said, in dialect.

The witch continued to say, 'I killed it, I didn't see it, I killed it.' Stopped only when she noticed him, his black habit standing out against the other people gathered around.

'Father, I killed it.'

The young priest leaned toward the cat and caressed its head. Then he grasped the bicycle and pulled it upright, without speaking. Rang the rusty bell, once.

# 2

The cafe was located on a corner opposite the condominium, across a cobbled street furrowed with the rails of two tram lines. There was little room inside, a few 1930s tables surrounded by assorted chairs and a whiff of cream, the walls covered with old film posters. Velvet lamps hung from the ceiling. The lawyer was seated in a blue armchair and reading a newspaper. He raised his eyes and saw the concierge. On the wall behind him was a black-and-white Anita Ekberg in the Trevi Fountain. Across the table sat Fernando and his mother, a petite woman smelling of hairspray. Her slim legs sprouted from a puff skirt. When Pietro entered she spun round in her seat.

'What a pleasant surprise!' She came forward to meet him, her wrinkled face framed by a perm. 'Please have a seat.' She pointed to the chair next to her.

The lawyer folded his newspaper and cleared his throat.

'So then, Pietro, in the end I convinced you! Welcome. In my capacity as condominium administrator, please allow me to introduce you to our Fernando and his mother, the charming Paola. Second floor, cherrywood door, next to the Martinis.'

Fernando kept his back turned, a felt beret pulled low on his head, his elbows planted either side of an empty cup. Stared at the black-haired barista behind the counter. Pietro greeted the boy, who grunted in reply. The first time he ever saw him, the day of his arrival at the condominium, he had been clinging to his mother's skirts as he repeated, 'I don't want to go to work, I want to stay with you.' He wore small round spectacles. He was twenty years old but also eighty.

'Fernando, say hello to Pietro.' His mother shook his shoulder and he brushed her hand away.

'He's in love and can't make up his mind to come out with it,' said the lawyer Poppi, rubbing his hands together. 'Dear Pietro, can I offer you a cappuccino with a sprinkle of cinnamon?'

'I'll have an espresso, thank you.'

'The specialty here is cappuccino with cinnamon. Alice makes them like no one else. Please try one.'

'That will be enough, Mr Poppi.' Fernando's mother fingered the string of pearls at her neck. 'How are you finding it with us, Pietro? Have you settled in?'

The concierge nodded.

The barista came toward them. She wore a fringe and the top two buttons of her shirt undone. She smiled at Pietro. 'Can I get you something?'

The lawyer elbowed him.

'A cappuccino,' said Pietro.

Fernando raised his head. His face was broad, his smooth cheeks inflamed.

'One cappuccino. Anything else, sir?'

'Yes,' the lawyer replied for him. 'On top of the cappuccino for my friend Pietro, could you draw' – he raised his voice – 'a cinnamon heart as only you, Alice, can?'

Paola turned toward her son. Fernando had straightened

up and sat poised on his seat. Then mumbled something incomprehensible and sank down limply on the table.

His mother stroked his face. 'Do you want to go home, Fernandello?' Stroked his face again. 'I'm taking you home.'

The lawyer smothered a laugh behind a handkerchief. ' He thinks she makes the heart in the cappuccino foam just for him.'

Paola turned back to them. 'You'll pay for this, Poppi, you cruel, cruel man.'

The lawyer winked and stood. He left two notes under the plate, kissed Fernando on the neck and walked out.

'He does things like that, but he's a good person,' said Paola, fussing with her wedding ring. 'It's only thanks to him that we received . . .' she whispered, 'the compensation.'

Pietro frowned.

'It's been five years now since my Gianfranco died. Seems like an eternity. He worked with asbestos for decades. If it hadn't been for Poppi, we wouldn't have seen a single cent.' She sighed. 'We are widow and widower, the two of us.'

Pietro looked at her.

'I'm sure you've seen the two names on the lawyer's letterbox. Daniele, that was his name. They spent a lifetime together.' She nodded to herself. 'I was left with my son. He was left with the condominium. That's why he worries about everyone, especially now . . .' She paused. 'I don't want to seem like a gossip.'

'You don't seem like a gossip.'

Alice served the cappuccino, a cinnamon heart at the

centre of the foam, a butter biscuit on the plate. Pietro placed the cup on Fernando's table.

The boy immediately began to drink, and Paola said, 'You know hot milk is bad for you, stop it now!' Then lowered her voice, 'I watch television in the kitchen, it was a habit my husband and I had. Unfortunately, our room shares a wall with Dr Martini's study, and walls talk. Things with them are not at all well.'

'I know that he lost his mother recently.'

Paola touched his hand lightly. 'Things with them are not at all well.' She shook her head, stopped, sniffed and sniffed again. 'Do you smell something too?'

The putrid odour came and went, overpowering when it did the whiff of cream. She leaned closer to her son. 'Fernando, stand up.'

Fernando was resting his chin on the palm of one hand and eyeing the barista as she cleaned the espresso machine. He said no and gulped down the last of the cappuccino.

'Fernando, stand up.' She bent over him. 'Hot milk is bad for you, not that you ever listen to me.' Tugged at him, helping him to his feet. 'Come on, honey, let's go home.'

Fernando pulled off his glasses. They swung from their cord and bounced on his chest. He looked down and shuffled like a penguin, Alice said bye, then he passed and only then did Pietro notice the dark halo staining his trousers. The stink had become unbearable. Paola tied her herringbone coat around her son's waist.

*

The witch was saying, Where did the cat's soul go, Father, tell me where it went. She hunched her shoulders and her voice could barely be heard.

'Come,' said the young priest, leading her through the crowd and into the church. Then he hurried to find the hydrogen peroxide and when he returned he disinfected the scratch. She flinched at the sting. She was beautiful like the year before and the year before that, with one ring more on her finger, something less in her eyes.

'Your cat is dead and I'm a witch because I killed it.' Her fleshy mouth trembled. She pressed a hand to her stomach.

'Does it hurt?'

'I'll go to hell.'

He continued to press the cotton to her knee, longer than necessary. Lifted his eyes to her chest swelling her dress.

'Your name's Celeste, isn't it?'

'I want to purge myself of this sin, Father.'

'You didn't see the cat.'

'I want to confess. In the confessional, right?' The witch stood and headed for the booth, did an about-turn and plucked some chewing gum from her mouth. 'If I talk with this in my mouth, will the Lord be offended?'

# 3

Pietro remained in the cafe. He had ordered a hot chocolate and waited for it to cool, enough for the slightly bitter film to form on top. Scooped it up with the spoon then dunked the two butter biscuits that Alice had brought on the side. He ate them as he drank, and as he drank he watched the condominium through the window. The Martinis had yet to return.

He paid at the register. As Alice gave him his change, she said, 'I feel bad for that boy Fernando. I never know how to act.' The concierge put the money in his pocket without counting it and went out. He crossed the street and passed into the courtyard of the condominium. A plaster Madonna in its alcove stood out against the ivy. The lawyer Poppi had asked to have it removed, but the residents refused. It had been there since the Second World War, a gesture of thanks for having spared the building from English bombs.

Pietro stepped up onto the rim of the mosaic-tiled basin and checked the ivy in the vicinity of the plastic halo. The snails were gone. He looked down. They had fallen near the plants that the residents had entrusted to him. He gathered up the snails and deposited them beneath a lemon tree and a flowering cactus.

'My gardenia is all dried up, I can feel it.'

Pietro turned around.

Viola Martini was at the entrance to the courtyard, toying

with a lock of honey-blonde hair and awaiting the verdict on tiptoe. 'It's dried up, isn't it?'

'Good afternoon,' said the concierge, attempting to smile. 'Give it a few more weeks and it will pull through.'

'You're a miracle worker, you are.' She bit her lip and came forward. 'How is it going, Pietro?' She winked at him and he smelled the scent of vanilla that lingered on the stairs each night.

Dr Martini stood further back, their daughter in his arms. Set her down and the child skipped over to the gardenia. Poking from her pocket was a pencil that was a magic wand. She drew it out like a small sword and touched Pietro on the head.

'What have you turned me into?' asked the concierge.

Sara scrunched up her coal-black eyes and slipped her head among the leaves of the gardenia, disappeared and re-appeared on the other side of the plant. Laughed from her gap-toothed mouth and stared at the snail in the pot. Touched the magic wand to its horns and the snail retreated. The child's face darkened.

'He's gone back into his shell to have a snack, honey,' said Dr Martini as he picked her up. Blew gently against her neck as his phone began to ring. Checked the display and immediately passed the girl to her mother. 'Hello, I'll call you back in five minutes.' Listened a moment. 'I said I'll call back in five minutes.' Hung up.

'Who was it?' asked Viola.

'The hospital.'

'You're going in tonight as well?'

The plants covered Pietro. Through the leaves the doctor's face was a sliver of sparse beard chewing gum. 'I'm not going, don't worry.' Then he turned to the concierge. 'Is there any post?'

Pietro went into the lodge as mother and daughter started up the stairs, leafed through the envelopes. 'There's a package and a registered letter. I'll need your signature.'

The doctor scribbled his name. 'My daughter adores you.' Held the gum between his teeth for a moment before returning to chewing. 'If you have this effect on all children, come and see me in the ward.' Screwed up his face in a grimace, the same as in the photograph on the Vespa. Drummed his fingers between an ashtray and the radio that the concierge had brought with him from the coast. Turned it on. His mobile phone rang again and he turned up the radio. The phone persisted and he picked it up. Before responding he stuck the chewing gum in the ashtray. 'Hello.' The doctor left the lodge. 'We agreed that I would call back.' He paused. 'Tonight I can't.'

The concierge turned off the radio. The doctor said, 'No, tonight I can't. I'm on tomorrow night at the hospital. I'll come over before, around seven. Yes, tomorrow. Don't call any more, it's risky. It's risky, I said.' The doctor was an attenuated shadow on the wall of the entrance hall. He put away his phone and rested a moment with a hand over his eyes. 'See you, Pietro. I'm going.'

'Have a good evening.' The concierge waited for him to go

up. Then went to the ashtray. *It's risky, I said.* Snatched up the doctor's chewing gum and went into the bedroom. In the suitcase there was also an old matchbox. He stuck the gum inside, beside another, rock-hard piece of gum.

# 4

Pietro had learned that they were looking for a concierge in Milan from the letter with the Emilio Salgari stamp. The postman delivered it one ordinary afternoon to his old address, an eighteenth-century church fronting on a piazza in Rimini. He put it into the hands of the servant, a wisp of a woman with shifty eyes and bow legs.

'I'll make sure he gets it,' she said. 'Don Pietro hasn't lived here for a year.' And she walked over to the old priest's new house.

'Padre.' She knocked three times. 'Padre.'

Pietro opened the door. 'I'm no longer Padre.' He returned to the living room.

'You are for me.' She pulled her shawl close and followed him in, leaving the letter on a folding bed in the living room.

There was no return address, just his name and the address of the church in anonymous cursive script. There was this stamp and the rice paper that shed invisible specks. Pietro opened it along the short side. Inside were a photograph and a sheet of paper folded in thirds. He pulled out the paper and began to read. Immediately stopped.

'Everything OK?' The servant had shuffled closer to him. 'Everything OK? Is it the woman?'

Pietro closed his eyes.

*

He had read it that evening, and again at night. Two times in all. The photograph, on the other hand, he never stopped looking at. He had followed the instructions: call some lawyer by the name of Poppi and set up an interview for the concierge job. He met him the next week in Milan, in this elegant but not pretentious condominium, and following their conversation returned to Rimini.

Three days later, sitting on a rock in the sea, he found out he would become a concierge.

The lawyer was the one to call him with the news. When Poppi heard the seagulls in the background he said, 'Pietro, you've got to be crazy to come to Milan to look after a condominium.' He revealed that in the interview Pietro's conservative haircut and a certain propensity for silence had been decisive. His past employment as a priest had elicited the agreement of all the residents except him. But majority ruled. Would he accept the job?

Pietro accepted, and before finishing they agreed when he would start.

Then the lawyer cleared his throat, 'Just out of curiosity, why did you divorce God?'

'He wasn't so easy to get along with.'

'You and I are going to be great friends. See you in four days.'

Pietro put away his phone and pulled out the letter on rice paper, squeezed it till he crumpled Salgari. Then passed by the church that had been his for a lifetime. In the piazza at the front, two old men greeted him. He continued without turning toward the walls that he had traded in for a tiny dump on the outskirts of the city. Three rooms in all, an equal number of pieces of luggage. The same ones that he would bring with him to Milan: two duffel bags and the suitcase with the boxes.

On the evening of his departure he abandoned the rest: shelves full of books and a drawer of Benedictine knick-knacks. With one bag on his back and the other in one hand, he laid the suitcase across the handlebars of the Bianchi and headed to the station. The train was on time. He bought his ticket and made a phone call.

'I'm coming tonight, Anita. They've hired me. Sorry about the last minute.'

# 5

In the notebook where he set down things not to forget, he wrote, *Dr Martini, at around seven tomorrow, then the hospital: risky*. He quickly closed it and went to the telephone on the shelf in the lodge, dialled the only number he knew by heart.

'Anita, I'm running late.'

He hung up and returned to the flat. One of the bags was on the kitchen table. He dumped out what had been left inside. At the bottom were crosswords and balled-up vests. He threw everything into the wardrobe, empty at the bottom except for two woollen jumpers and some worn shoes, and removed from a hanger the only outfit hanging there, a black suit and white shirt. The jacket had mother-of-pearl buttons and the trousers were cuffless. He kept his good shoes under the bed in a plastic bag. Pulled them out now and rummaged through a dresser drawer. The skinny tie was stuffed against the box of earplugs. He smoothed it between his palms. Dressed hurriedly and wheeled out the Bianchi. As he emerged from the condominium he found a petrol-blue SUV parked up on the pavement.

'Oh, good evening, Pietro.' Poppi the lawyer was leaning against the vehicle door. A thin man stood beside him. 'May I introduce you to Dr Riccardo Lisi? Radiographer and a good friend of the Martinis.'

The two men moved away from the SUV and Pietro noticed that the door had a scratch and two large dents.

'We've already met.' The radiographer wore an open raincoat. Extended his hand toward the concierge. 'We ran into each other on the day you first arrived. Three bags and that Bianchi, wasn't it?' Pointed at it and brushed the hair away from his face. His eyes were grey.

'That's right, Dr Lisi.'

'Riccardo. *Dr Lisi* makes me feel old. Do you have a lock for it?'

'It's broken.'

'They pinch Bianchis in Milan. May I?' He grabbed the bicycle, climbed on and leaned over the handlebars as if he were hurtling down a hill. 'They don't make 'em like this any more. I've got one myself, but it's made of tissue paper.'

'Do you ride it?'

'I used to, with that wimp Martini. Then he defected and I get bored riding on my own.'

'You two could go riding together.' The lawyer opened his arms wide.

'Resolved.' Riccardo gave the bicycle back to Pietro. 'You've got to be patient, though. I don't have the legs I once did.' He started up the stairs.

He had left behind the scent of aftershave, sickly sweet, which mixed with the smog.

'I've seen him around a lot lately,' said Pietro.

'You see him around a lot lately, right.' Poppi raised his eyebrows. 'Let's say that he's one of the family. He was at university with Dr Martini and now they work in the same hospital. The little girl calls him "Uncle".' He looked Pietro up and down. 'I admit the white shirt does wonders for you,

Pietro.' He adjusted the concierge's tie and opened the door to the building. 'Who's the lucky woman tonight?'

Pietro started off.

'Don't be coy. What's her name?'

'Anita.'

'I was thinking Mary Magdalene. Good for you, kibitzer. God will be jealous tonight.'

The concierge stood stiffly on the threshold of the flat. Anita said, 'You have the same face as when you first arrived in Milan.' She pulled him inside. 'C'mon, tell me. Are you worried about something?'

Pietro leaned against the new refrigerator. Its door was already covered with recipes. She caressed the two creases around his mouth. 'If these wrinkles . . .' Moved on to the furrows on his forehead. 'And these . . .' Finished with the groove in his chin. 'And this as well . . . have shown up, something has happened.' Helped him out of his jacket, then checked on a pot heating on the stove. 'Knowing you this long has got to mean something.'

Pietro turned to the window. It looked over a communal balcony into the tenement's courtyard. A string of petunias hung down from the balustrade. He managed to make out the Bianchi. 'Sorry I'm late.' He sat down, and only now did he notice that Anita was different.

'You're worried,' she said.

Her lips were shiny and she wore pearls at her earlobes. Her hair was freshly dyed a shade approaching auburn. Her dress hugged wide hips partially concealed by a hanging scarf.

'You're beautiful,' Pietro replied. And he gazed at the old photograph on the wall of her on the Rimini breakwater. She held her hat to keep it from blowing away and she was happy.

She lowered her eyes. 'I went by your building this morning.' Used a wooden spoon to scoop up a bit of *ragù* from the pot. The sauce was simmering over a low flame. She cooled it down with a long breath before placing it in her mouth. 'The condominium is very distinguished, but I didn't see the doctor.'

'He had already left at that hour.'

'I saw a blonde woman and a little girl.'

'His wife and daughter.'

'If they're any guide, the doctor is one handsome man.' She caressed his ringless fingers. 'Have you spoken to him?'

Pietro sprang to his feet. On the sideboard stood a glass amphora. Anita had filled it with coloured buttons and decks of cards. He pulled out the *briscola* cards. They were worn at the edges, the images faded. He began to shuffle them. 'Today I used my set of keys to go into his flat.'

'When?'

'This afternoon.'

She pushed aside plate and silverware. 'Goodness, and then?'

'I saw a photograph.' Pietro shuffled the cards and spoke softly. 'He liked Vespas when he was little. After that I had to leave.'

Anita slipped the cards out of his hand and had him cut the deck. Then turned them over two by two: the three of cups and the six of coins, the king and the ace of cups. 'The cards say you'll go back. Back to his flat. Because he'll need you.'

Pietro looked over her shoulder. The ace of cups had been the first card dealt. He put an arm around Anita like he had done after climbing down from the Rimini–Milan train, the day when they first saw each other again after ten years. She'd brought him home with her, to a comfortable two-room flat in a big ugly building north of the city. And he had slept there ever since: the four nights before becoming a concierge and virtually every night following.

Anita blew gently in his ear, loosened his tie.

He turned his head, buried his nose in her hair.

# 6

He woke with a start.

Anita, beside him, said, 'You had a nightmare, come here.'

Pietro caressed her head. 'I have to go.'

He went to the kitchen and drank from a glass with a hand-painted lizard on it. The green ran outside the lines of the pointed tail. He dressed and before leaving noticed that she was up, wearing a light dressing gown and gazing at him. 'He'll need you,' she said to him again.

Pietro crossed the room to embrace her, then left.

The night had swallowed Milan, swallowed him as well as the Bianchi carried him home. Traces of the nightmare stayed with him during the entire return trip. It was always the same. A ship and the salty air, with no sea beneath the ship, just emptiness. And his fall from the bows, down, down, until he woke. He banished it by pedalling, pedalling without stopping all the way to the condominium. Such was his frenzy that he struggled to insert the keys into the building door. Left the Bianchi against the downpipe at the entrance to the courtyard, calming down once he was there, his gaze directed at the doctor's windows. They were dark. In one he could make out the ceiling beams and a chandelier with many arms. The beams and the chandelier were enough for him. *You will need me*. A darkened window was enough. He returned towards the concierge's lodge and just before entering noticed something on the ground, a leather bracelet. Picked it up. It was frayed at the edges and smooth on top. On the underside a date had been etched: *14-9-2008*. He placed it in the drawer of his night table.

Then the concierge took off his suit, hung the shirt and jacket in the wardrobe, chose a red tracksuit as pyjamas. Instead of the bed he would make do with a blanket and a mothball-smelling pillow inherited from the previous concierge. Picked up too a crossword puzzle and a pen, then removed his socks and went into the empty room. There was a musty odour that rose from the filthy floor. Three of the walls had been recently painted white, the fourth left half plastered, sign that the work had been interrupted. He opened the porthole window that looked into the courtyard and turned on the lamp. What remained of memory? Pietro stood frozen, staring at the suitcase. Only things. He bent down to open a box, removed a note and read it against the light. The writing in pencil had faded but he could nevertheless make it out: *I killed my son*. With note in hand he stood and rocked back onto his heels, shifted onto his toes and sketched a graceful tap dance. Stopped. What remained of memory? He brought a hand under the lamp. Against the half-plastered wall he projected the shadows of his fingers, held them together and then spread them open, closed, open again. They became a dog without a tail. He had learned how to make the shadows as a young man. Now they were lopsided and a few were always missing something. He moved his index finger and thumb. The dog opened his jaw. To the animal he confided: 'Tomorrow night at seven, I'll follow him.'

*

The eyes of the witch sparkled through the confessional grille. She murmured in a Milanese accent, 'Where'd it go, Father, the cat's soul? And mine, where'll it go? I have to get married soon. How can I do it with my soul so troubled, how?'

'Do you pray?'

'I write to him, to God.'

They were silent. He heard her moving behind the grille. She drew something from her handbag, tore off a strip of paper and pulled out a pencil she had been using to keep her hair in place. Wrote on the paper and pushed it through.

The words written on the paper were: *I have another sin to confess, God, but I can't say it to you, only write it.*

He handed the paper back to her. 'Do it.'

And she wrote it with gaunt *i*s and *l*s and a portly *o*: *I killed my son.*

# 7

Pietro slept poorly owing to the hard floor and the odour of mothballs that stung his nose. He woke at first light.

The floor was frigid. He placed his feet on top of the socks there and reread the only crossword clue that he had been unable to solve, five across, three letters: *ruminant with palmate antlers*. He wrote *elk* and went into the bathroom to undress. Over the years his torso had shrunk. The hair remained dark on his slight paunch. He caressed it softly, the skin that of a newborn. Unscrewed the cap on the body wash for sensitive skin and turned on the shower, a square of floor separated by a plastic curtain. As soon as it became lukewarm he started on his legs. They were a runner's legs. Disfiguring scars ran over his thighs and shins. He traced them with two fingers, down to his small feet, which he scrubbed. He had prominent veins and scars on his ankles as well. Poured out more body wash, soaped his face and felt the bubbles bursting on his nose. They didn't smell like anything. He inhaled and his nostrils burned. Held one hand to his wrinkly member, grasped it and fingered the tip. Stopped and stared at that strip of flesh. Rinsed it with cold water and rinsed the cuts that crossed his chest from one side to another. His bones slid under the tortured skin that still hurt at times. He opened the plastic curtain and before stepping out looked at himself in the mirror behind the door. He was a man reddened by the hot water and by memory.

He did the rest in a hurry. Chose a shirt and trousers and an argyle jumper that he threw over his shoulders. He had bought them in Anita's shop the day before starting the job. He had chosen the colour, grey, she the style, and she had also made him buy an uncomfortable pair of brogues and two cardigans to alternate, because a proper concierge almost never dresses the same two days in a row. Anita had also added a tie and a bottle of cologne, which he had yet to open. Pietro pulled on the jumper, adjusted his shirt collar and went into the kitchen without stopping to look in the mirror. A colour other than black was enough to embarrass him.

Pietro had always eaten breakfast on his feet. He set up on top of the refrigerator, with exactly two pieces of Melba toast and three squares of dark chocolate. Ate slowly, eyes on the plants awaiting the morning light. 'You tricked me,' he said to a recovering ficus that he had given up for lost. Placed it more squarely in the sun's path and went into the lodge. Checked the notebook with the list of things to remember. Dr Martini's daughter's birthday was just a week away. Nicolini the magician would be stopping by in the next few days to work out where to do the show. The concierge would first have to clean out the gutters and prune the hedge. He stood to open the lodge window's curtains, instead returned to the bedroom and took the keys to the Martinis'.

Pietro carried the keys in his pocket and occasionally felt to be sure they were still there. He had to wait until the building emptied. The first to leave was the lawyer. On pool days he was always an early riser. Shortly after it was Paola's turn. She came up to the lodge.

'My Fernando is ill and won't be going to work today.' The smell of hairspray struck him full in the face. 'Would you mind looking in on him every so often?'

Pietro nodded. 'I'll also drop off this cactus. It's better.'

'I'll pay you back with dinner.' Paola put on her hat and went out as the voice of the doctor's daughter floated down the stairwell. Sara whimpered, cuddled up against her mother's chest, an invisible bundle with one eye open wide, the other closed. Waved the magic wand and stared at him.

Viola put her down. 'She doesn't want to go to nursery school. What am I to do?' She buttoned up the girl's hooded top. 'Have a good day, Pietro.' Smiled and went out with her daughter.

The postman came early. Pietro sped up operations by telling him he would distribute the post to the boxes himself. The postman handed over the lot and the concierge set to work. For Paola there was a fashion magazine with the newest collections and a current-affairs weekly that was mostly gossip. He had come across the previous issue in the wastepaper bin and read it during quiet times. He flipped through this one briefly then continued to pick through the pile. There were also three envelopes for Fernando's mother, two of them still addressed to her husband. He put them in her box. For the lawyer there was a newsletter from the Rotary club and a child sponsorship update. Remaining on the table was the post for the Martinis. Viola had received an invitation to an art opening. He placed it in their box and turned to the doctor's post. There was an envelope from a medical conference and the *Corriere della Sera,* which he came to the lodge every morning to pick up. Pietro removed the plastic wrapper and refolded the newspaper carefully so that the corners were perfectly matched. He spied a front-page article about a Mafioso on the run being arrested, had begun to read it when the doctor came down. With a gym bag over his shoulder and a phone to his ear, the doctor signed to him that he would pick up the paper later. Pietro waited until he left, then checked the time.

He entered the courtyard. Viola's gardenia was still in low spirits, Paola's cactus revived and beginning to flower. He picked up the latter and carried it into the entrance hall. The stairs were silent as a tomb. He began to climb, staggering with the weight of the cactus until the first floor, where he had to pause before continuing up. No sound came from the doors on the second floor. He moved closer to Poppi's door and heard the low murmur of the television that the lawyer left on every time he went out, put down the cactus on the Martinis' doormat and rang the bell. Rang again. Drew out the keys, inserted them into the locks and opened the door.

The photograph of the doctor on the Vespa was as he had left it. He lifted it up and noticed that the child was clutching something in his less visible hand, perhaps a slingshot, perhaps just a piece of rope. Beside the picture frame the basket of knick-knacks appeared piled high even without the bell. He went over to the hall stand and brought his nose to a black trench coat. It smelled of vanilla. He stopped sniffing and lifted his head.

In the middle of the room were two red couches set at right angles. Bookshelves covered the long wall and surrounded the door to the kitchen. More books strewed the floor. As he stepped over them he read *The Razor's Edge* on one cover. He walked around. The little girl's toys crowded the carpet. Some dolls sat up on a chaise longue beneath the window.

Through the glass he could see the courtyard, a bit of the Madonna and an arc of his porthole window. He continued to wander, the parquet floor squeaked, he slowed his steps and arrived at a pair of men's slippers beside a couch. Sat down, took off his shoes and put on the slippers. Wiggled his toes, working them all the way in. They fitted him perfectly. As his feet warmed up Pietro approached the one wall painted crimson. On the right hung a photograph of a lavender field. Among the flowers appeared the doctor and Viola in an embrace, perhaps from when they were at university. He ran a finger along the outline of the pale young man with a patchy beard and a lavender flower over one ear. Viola was looking at the camera and he was looking at her. They were beautiful. On the mantel he spotted their wedding picture: she full of soft curves in her white gown, he a mannequin in morning dress. Another photograph was of the doctor arm in arm with Riccardo, the radiographer, their faces deformed with laughter. A final one showed a man in sunglasses holding a fishing rod, a fish hanging from two fingers. He knew it was the doctor's father, who had died a few years back.

The voice of Fernando came through the wall, 'Papa and Jesus, I will offend you no more.' Then silence.

Pietro went into the kitchen. A bouquet of sunflowers hung down from the wall above the table, a card pinned to the paper: *To Viola, who passes beneath the windows*. He read the doctor's signature. The *a* in *Luca* had a long, curly tail. A shelf held an aquarium with striped tropical fish. Beside it a long, narrow loaf of bread poked out of its bag. He pressed a finger against a crumb and put it in his mouth. The bread was fresh. Then he stood in front of the refrigerator. On the door were a magnet shaped like the Eiffel Tower and a black-and-white Polaroid, the ultrasound of Sara in her mama's belly. He ran his finger slowly over it, recognizing the upturned nose and little round head, caressed it and noticed a handwritten date in the lower right corner: 14-9-2008. The same as the bracelet found in the courtyard. He pressed the corners down and heard another voice, of the lawyer this time: 'Theo Morbidelli, where are you? No swimming today because your owner doesn't feel so good. I'm going into the bathroom, so kindly get out of the way, c'mon now . . .'

Pietro checked his watch, went back into the sitting room, and slid open a door leading to the bedrooms. He passed the little girl's room: the walls were plastered with drawings; a pink quilt covered the bed; a stuffed Winnie the Pooh sat atop the pillow. He continued down the corridor to the last room, the one sharing a wall with Fernando's sitting room, the doctor's study. A laptop peeked out beneath piles of papers and books on the desk. The leather armchair was buried in old newspapers. A stringless guitar rested on a stand. On the wall he saw the doctor's diploma. He walked around the desk and touched the frame, read *with the highest distinction* and pressed his fingers against the glass. Held them there, then stooped over the desk. Some doodled sheets of paper and a bowl of grape stems. He crouched down in front of the three drawers below the work surface.

He undid a button of his shirt and felt his throat pulsing. Pulled open the first drawer. Inside were a packet of liquorice gum, a mobile-phone charger, a pile of cotton handkerchiefs, a leather-bound diary. He closed the drawer. A cascade of water roared in the pipes in the wall and muddied the lawyer's voice: 'Here I am, Theo, I'm fine now. Come here and give me some love.'

He reopened the drawer and paged through the diary. On the first page there was nothing. On the others he read last names, account numbers, payment due dates, more doodles. He went to 8 February, the day of the death of the doctor's mother. The page was blank. On the next, scrawled diagonally across the page: *No frame, Mama, just the memory.*

He paged ahead and noticed that some dates were circled in pen, 9 January several times. Underneath, a line: *How will you condemn me, God?* He paused. Read again: *How will you condemn me, God?* Continued to flip through. The third of May was circled as well and bore the same message. He searched the surface of the desk, found a blank piece of paper and a pen, traced the doctor's handwriting. Folded up the paper and placed it in his pocket. Checked the coming days, pages full of reminders about Sara's birthday party. The order placed with the pastry shop Madame La Cuisine, the magician Massimo Nicolini's expenses.

He opened to today's date. It was circled. The doctor had

noted, *7:00, call first,* and lower down, *Don't have the courage.* Pietro stared at the writing.

The second drawer was locked. He shook it and something moved inside. The third was unlocked. He slid it open and a jumble of photographs appeared, on top one of a woman holding a newborn in her arms, her face pressed against the sleeping child, her smile that of someone in her twenties.

He closed the drawer quickly and left the study. When he came to the Martinis' bedroom he leaned against the door jamb, then shuffled slowly to the wicker bed and bent down over the two orange pillows. He sank his face into the pillowcase with the smell of Luca.

This time he breathed.

# 8

Pietro slowly closed the door to the Martinis' flat and instinctively turned to where the lawyer had surprised him the last time. Saw the giant window above the landing wide open, a stream of light dazzling the cream walls. Picked the cactus up off the doormat and took two steps toward Fernando's door. Froze. The door was ajar and through the gap poked a loafer.

'You stole.' Fernando was there. The door of the flat opened completely. Now there were two loafers. They came forward, below pyjama bottoms with elasticated bands stretched around fleshy calves. 'You stole.'

'I was bringing back your plant, Fernando. It's better now.' Pietro called him over but the strange boy took no heed.

Fernando moved slowly in the thick pyjamas. 'How do you know it's better?'

'It made flowers. Come and see how pretty they are.'

He shook his head.

It was the first time Pietro had ever seen him without the beret. His hair was short, thinning in the middle and speckled with grey. 'Come and see, we won't say anything to your mother.' He pointed out the bud of a reddish flower.

Fernando hesitated, then took a quick look. 'Mama says you heal the plants with prayers.' He cleaned the toe of one shoe with a thumb.

The concierge put the cactus back down on the mat.

'When all the flowers bloom you can give it to Alice at the cafe. She'll be happy.'

The strange boy thought about it. 'Happy.' He smiled and seized the concierge's hand, crushing the fingers with his oxlike strength.

Pietro tried to break away but Fernando refused to let him. The boy drew him into the dimly lit entryway, dragged him into a living room that also contained a kitchen. The shutters were rolled down and the only light came from a small table with five cemetery candles placed in a circle. In the middle lay his felt beret.

The boy took a folded blanket from the couch and placed it at the foot of the table beside another blanket. He knelt down and made a sign for the concierge to do the same.

'Say a prayer for Papa.'

Pietro stayed on his feet. He watched the strange boy's broad back collapse toward the altar, return upright, collapse again. Abruptly he ceased to move, a graceless statue.

'Lie down on the couch, you're tired,' said the concierge.

He did not obey.

'Lie down.'

He remained motionless.

So Pietro picked up the blanket, opened and laid it across the boy's shoulders. Backed away without taking his eyes off this son at prayer.

The witch crouched in the corner of the confessional, *I killed my son,* crushed her face up against the grille.

'My baby never saw the light of day. An old nurse and I, we snuffed him out.'

'He has seen the eternal light.' The young priest moved closer.

She pulled back. 'You priests always say the same thing.'

'It's called faith.'

'Faith . . . Tell it to someone who's given birth to a sin.' She moved away as far as possible.

'Why did you kill him?'

'Give me this faith as well.' The witch ran out.

The young priest called after her, called her again, watched her leave the church. Then he exited the confessional and knelt down on the wood where she had knelt. And instead of praying he gathered up the single long hair left behind in the grille, held it in his left hand.

Directly he returned home Pietro poured himself half a glass of red wine from the bottle he had brought from Rimini. It had gone sour. He drank it quickly, held it against his palate until it sweetened, closed his eyes and that was his prayer for Fernando.

He swallowed when he heard knocking at the lodge window. The shiny head of the lawyer emerged out of a cloud of smoke. Poppi had a cigar in his mouth and a dressing gown cinched at his waspish waist. Pietro slid open the lodge window.

'Pietro,' he said, 'have you seen one of the Martinis come in?'

The acidic wine rose from his stomach.

'No.'

'Then there's something funny going on. This morning when I got to the pool, I didn't even have time to change before my bowels started sounding the alarm – I imagine it's retribution for having taken the mick out of Fernando at the cafe. I went straight back home and in the bathroom Theo Morbidelli and I heard suspicious sounds. Do you like Theo Morbidelli as a cat's name?'

Pietro nodded.

'Anyway, at a certain point Theo Morbidelli and I heard a sound coming from the doctor's office. Where were you, kibitzer?'

'I took Fernando the cactus. We talked for a while outside his door.'

'Ah. Maybe it was you . . .' The lawyer bit his lips. 'It's just that I'm always on the lookout.'

'You're a good administrator.'

Poppi put out the cigar and pushed his way into the lodge. 'Ever since his mother kicked the bucket the doctor has lost his head. A good administrator . . . A nurse is more like it.'

The concierge sat down.

The lawyer's voice softened. 'He got his bearings in life from his mother.' He settled down next to Pietro and for the first time Pietro got a good look at him. Poppi was a tired man with tiny watery eyes who refused to surrender to old age. He gestured with his hands, let them fall to his lap and continued: 'And now that the bearings are lost, the ship has no direction.' He opened the dressing gown slightly, revealing his scrawny chest. 'In the evenings he's out of the house a lot, and I've heard Viola crying more than once since the kid was born. I've heard him crying too. He sounds like a crow when he cries.'

'Maybe the crows don't want to be listened to.'

'We should have thicker walls.'

'Or more discreet tongues.'

The lawyer turned his back on the concierge. 'Maybe you, Pietro, still have God to keep you company and don't need anyone else' – he crossed his legs – 'but let me tell you a story, my friend. When my mother found out that I was a poof, she said that I would be condemned to die alone like one other category of people: priests.' His eyes now were dry and growing in size. 'My mother was right, except in one point, if I may: we homos are buried without any desires left, you priests with your mouths still spouting sermons.' He chewed on the extinguished cigar.

Pietro was silent.

Poppi feigned blowing smoke. 'Did you know you've got no sense of humour?' Then he laid a hand on the concierge's knee and squeezed. 'Pardon me.' He bowed his bony head. He once again appeared tired, his arms like twigs and his face fearful. He looked through the lodge window. 'I promised the doctor's mother that I would look out for him. Seeing him like this upsets me.'

Pietro looked through the lodge window as well, saw the geometric designs that decorated the ceiling of the entrance hall. Then a half-flowering cactus came lumbering its way past the lodge, with drooping arms and a trunk inclined to one side. The lawyer jumped to his feet and stared. They heard a buzz and a click.

'Jesus. Come and see this, Pietro.'

The half-flowering cactus swayed in the arms of Fernando as he tried unsuccessfully to open the door. He had on his beret and a corduroy shirt.

The lawyer closed his dressing gown and ran out of the lodge.

'Where do you think you're going?' He kept the door closed with his foot.

'Alice is happy with pretty flowers.'

'What?'

'Alice is happy.'

Pietro helped steady the cactus in the boy's arms. 'It's not completely flowered yet. We have to wait because like this it's not a nice gift.'

Poppi put an arm around Fernando.

'Let's go home, son.'

'Alice wants pretty flowers.'

'And we'll bring them to her. At the right moment, that is. With women it takes patience. Listen to someone who knows about these things.'

Poppi led Fernando and his cactus upstairs. Before disappearing he looked towards Pietro for an instant.

The concierge looked towards him as well. Then he slipped into the lodge and into the flat. Went into the bedroom, turned on the light and drew from his suitcase a rectangular box containing a plastic bag. It looked empty. He held it up to the light and saw what remained of a long hair, an invisible filament. Inside he also put the paper with the writing copied from the doctor's office, *How will you condemn me, God?*

Then he said to himself: 'Tonight at seven o'clock.'

# 9

The whole afternoon Pietro had fiddled with a wheel on the Bianchi that was slightly out of true. A patched inner tube was also slowly losing air and needed to be replaced. As he put the bike back together he saw the entire second floor gradually returning, in last place Viola, who hurried past without greeting him.

At six Pietro shut the lodge door and sat down, continuing nonetheless to monitor a slice of the entry through a gap in the curtains. He worked on a crossword puzzle in pen as he waited, solved four clues across and two down. Then, at ten minutes past six, he saw him. The doctor passed through the entrance hall and exited the condominium. Crossed the street to enter Alice's cafe, drank something at the counter against the backdrop of Mastroianni from *8½*, paid at the register. When he left, the concierge followed him at a distance. The doctor pushed through the evening air with bowed head, leather medical bag in hand and a blue jacket over his shoulder. He was a reed, his gait slow and princely. Pietro had been introduced to him by the lawyer on his first day at work. He had been in his lodge for an hour when Poppi knocked, beside him this polite and largely silent young man. Pietro had kept his gaze down, the doctor's on the rusty Bianchi. 'Big cyclist?' he had asked. 'I am,' the concierge had replied. They had shaken hands and Pietro had held on to that handshake all evening.

The doctor continued down the boulevard lined with acacia trees, stopped in front of a closed pastry shop and gazed at the Sachertorten on display. Opened his leather bag and drew out a piece of paper, read it and put it back, then brought his phone to his ear. As he started to walk again the wind lifted the jacket from his shoulder. He put it on. It was cool out, not night and hardly evening. The doctor passed the church of Sant'Andrea and its bell rang half-past six. At the last peal he looked up at the statue of a saint on the parapet. The concierge looked at the saint as well. When they lowered their eyes the mist had risen.

The glittering moist air isolated them. The doctor became a vague shadow speaking on the phone, stepping off the pavement and very nearly dropping his bag. He took the road to the hospital but continued on past the entrance. At five minutes to seven he turned into a sycamore-lined street that ran along the railway.

The mist dissipated. Martini left faint footprints in the fallen leaves as he slowed in front of an ugly greenish building with closed shutters and a series of informal garden plots in front. In the most kempt stood two pomegranate trees without fruit. Pietro hid himself behind a sycamore. The doctor pressed a button on the intercom and a light went on two floors above. A short while later a young woman appeared in the garden, fussed with the gate latch. She wore her dark hair pulled back in a bun and walked quickly. The doctor followed her, resting a hand on her back before disappearing into the building.

Pietro pressed himself up against the sycamore, feeling

cold. Rubbed his shoulders, huddled up to the tree and leaves fell around him. When he looked at the branches he saw that they were bare. On the thickest branch a long-haired cat was scratching its claws, stretching and scratching. It scratched one last time and stared at Pietro with yellow eyes. The concierge was unable to tear his gaze away from the beast. Meanwhile the cold came to his scars. They hurt. He grazed the biggest one, on his ankle, and collapsed against the sycamore. Sank down to the base of the trunk and stayed like that until the young woman walked the doctor back to the gate, forty minutes later. She reopened the latch and exchanged a few more words with him. Her hair was loose now. She brushed it away from her forehead with a graceful gesture and rested her hand on a statue of Snow White just outside the gate. Caressed the plaster head and spoke to the doctor. She herself resembled Snow White. Was Snow White. When she went back inside, the doctor hurried into the street and stopped abruptly beneath a street lamp, covered his face with his hands. Moved on with Pietro behind him.

The doctor arrived at the ward some time before eight. Pietro waited between two parked cars across the street. The hospital was a citadel rising out of the darkness, with the illuminated accident and emergency department and six other buildings scattered among fir trees, an artificial lake to one side.

Pietro went through the gate and started down the path between fir trees, reached the building with the sign reading *Paediatric Oncology*. The neon light at the entrance flickered. Through the windows passed the faint echo of treble voices.

They came from the profiles of people behind half-open windows. He entered. Climbed the first flight of stairs and the neon light went out. Climbed a second set and as the neon glared again he found the doctor. Kneeling with his back to Pietro, he was draping his jacket over a child.

'And you wanted to go to the lake now?' he was saying. 'In your pyjamas?'

Of the little boy only a sliver of gleaming head could be seen. The doctor kept him wrapped in the fabric and massaged his hips, did up the buttons on the jacket and it became an elegant cloak. The boy pulled his head all the way through and flashed deep blue eyes. He noticed Pietro, watched him without saying a word.

'*Ciao.*'

Dr Martini turned around.

Pietro raised a hand. '*Ciao.*'

The child stepped forward in his elegant cloak, holding tight to a book with two elephants on the cover titled *The Animals of the Savannah*.

'Lorenzo, this is my friend Pietro.' The doctor picked him up. 'So you really did come by to visit us.'

The concierge pointed to the book. 'Do you know what elephants do to spray water on themselves?'

The child brought a hand to his nose and that became his trunk.

'Good boy.'

'Today this so-called good boy made me angry.' The doctor beckoned Pietro to follow and opened the glass door to the ward. 'And now little Lorenzo is heading straight to bed; if not he'll catch a cold.' As he led the way in he addressed a nurse. 'He was on his way to the lake. That's the second time he's slipped by you.'

In the cramped waiting room a floor lamp threw light on three hot-air balloons painted on the wall and some crayon drawings pinned to a bulletin board.

'Now why don't you show Pietro your book?'

He settled the child on a chair and went to speak to a women waiting beside the yellow hot-air balloon. Lorenzo flipped through the book and turned towards the large window overlooking the lake. He was a poor little mite.

Pietro approached him. 'Have you ever seen an animal of the savannah?'

The child continued to seek out the lake beyond the glass, shook his head.

'I have.' The concierge crouched down and extended his arms beneath the lamp. Beside it on the wall appeared a lump of shadow the size of a football. It turned more vague, out-of-focus, then became two elephant ears.

The book fell from Lorenzo's hands.

And from the shadowy ears of the elephant appeared tusks and a trunk. It was enormous. It was tiny. It swelled and ran forward and back, lifted up its tusks.

Lorenzo's mouth dropped open. He edged forward on his seat. The greyness in his cheeks was gone. He stammered, stammered more loudly.

'What is it, little guy?' The doctor stepped over to him and picked up the picture book.

The child continued to stare at the concierge. Martini picked him up.

'I think it's time for beddy-bye.' He attempted a smile but his mouth failed to follow through. In place of his eyes there were two slits. 'Today's not a great day for visits. Come by another time if you can.'

'Bye, Lorenzo.' Pietro pushed open the glass door but did not go. 'Doctor,' he said, 'do you ever do house calls?'

'How do you mean?'

'House calls.'

'I haven't for a long time. Do you need anything?'

'You never know,' said the concierge. 'See you tomorrow.' He headed down the stairs, blinded by the neon lights. As he descended he held on to the handrail and to the memory of the doctor in the white coat and the child in the elegant cloak, of Snow White and the house of the pomegranate trees.

The path through the fir trees was a dark stripe. Standing astride it was an old man, half ghost and half scarecrow. 'Are they letting people in?' he asked. The man was more withered than a fallen fruit and wore the jacket and cap of a petrol pump attendant, both with the word *Total*. He brought his ravaged, crêpe-paper face closer. 'I have to talk to Dr Martini. Are they letting people in or not?' He coughed.

Pietro said no and slipped past him.

# 10

Before Pietro could make it back inside the condominium he heard his name called from above. He raised his head: the lawyer was balancing on the parapet and motioning for the concierge to join him at once.

Pietro continued to stare up at him from the street. Come down, he indicated, but Poppi wouldn't listen. The concierge entered and made directly for the stairs, hanging on to the handrail up to the second floor, where he had to slow down to catch his breath. Proceeded to the third and to the fourth. On the fifth there were skylights and an iron door that didn't lock. The door was heavy and half rusted and it screeched as he pulled it towards him. It opened onto the communal terrace, a square of concrete crowded with satellite dishes and a labyrinth of clotheslines. He stepped outside, peered around. There on the raised section of the roof toward the front of the building was Poppi, wrestling with a satellite dish and cursing. Then the lawyer stepped up again onto the parapet wall, trying to straighten the dish from the feed arm. Swaying from side to side, he had the balance of a wading bird and a small torch between his teeth. He now directed it at Pietro and muttered something.

'Mr Poppi, get down from there!' The concierge went over to him.

The lawyer pulled the torch from his mouth. 'This thing won't get any channels. I can't see a thing.' Managed to shift the dish slightly. He wore an overcoat over pyjamas, zigged and zagged in satin slippers. 'Do you know anything about satellite dishes?'

Pietro seized one of the man's calves and it felt to him like a shrivelled balloon. 'No. Come down.'

'I'm surprised, given what you're able to pick up.' He cursed again, then threw up his hands in a sign of surrender. Stayed on the wall and gave a kick to the dish.

The concierge helped him down. They sat and regained their breath. The lawyer wiped his forehead and switched off the torch, turning them into two more scraps of darkness. They became visible again for a moment when Poppi lit a cigarette.

'In the evenings, a broken satellite dish can hurt more than a divorce.'

The bed sheets flapped on the lines. Pietro watched them for a time, then turned to the street. The cafe was still open and through the window he could see two men at a table drinking beer. A tram was at the stop and a line of cars was forming beyond the traffic light. Crossing at the light were Paola and Fernando. The strange boy was weighed down with bags of groceries and followed his mother over the stripes.

'Are you afraid of heights, kibitzer?'

Pietro shook his head.

'Then you should come up here more often.' He ashed into the void. 'Up here is closer to your god.' With his cigarette he pointed at the sky. 'And to the movements of your residents.' He pointed at Fernando, about to enter the building. 'Do you know why he always wears that beret? It was his father's. He gave it to him not long before passing on to a worse life.' He blew a smoke ring. 'A warning: never touch it. Another warning: be more careful when you decide to clean the Martinis' flat top to bottom.'

Pietro leaned toward the lawyer. 'It was a moment of weakness . . .' He stood. 'It won't happen again.'

'Ah, but I love a good top-to-bottom cleaning too, my friend.' Poppi was nodding. 'And I can assure you that from up here they turn out better.' The lawyer was still staring down at the street. Fernando and Paola were coming in, the tram had continued on, the two men were still seated at their table at the cafe. 'They turn out much better, believe me,' he repeated as if speaking to himself, looking just past the cafe to the beginning of a one-way street. Pietro followed Poppi's gaze to a petrol-blue SUV, pulled over with its headlights on, its right side dented. He didn't immediately recognize it. The passenger door was ajar and the dome light on. Inside were the radiographer and Viola. They were smiling. She made to get out and Riccardo held her back. They laughed.

The lawyer flicked his cigarette butt down off the building. 'I'm the one who's afraid of heights.'

That night the witch threw a pebble at the young priest's window.

'Father, I dreamt about my son and your cat. Father, wake up.'

He was already awake. He turned over on his other side and closed his eyes.

'I dreamt about my son.'

The young priest clutched the sheet, yanked it, then got out of bed and went to the window, cracked it open. The witch was wrapped in a headscarf, numb with cold.

'Can I come in?'

'Go home.'

'So it isn't true that the house of the Lord is always open?'

The young priest descended to the ground floor and went through a side entrance to the church. He did up the last button of his nightshirt and opened the front door.

The witch came toward him.

'I dreamt of my son. He was playing with your cat.' She laughed. 'You look good in pyjamas.' She removed her headscarf and let her hair down, took two steps which were one. Arrived at the votive altar and picked up a new candle.

'Tell the Lord why you killed your son.'

'It's a secret.'

'He keeps everyone's secrets.'

The witch lit the candle and reserved the first bit of melting wax for herself, dripping it onto the back of her hand. 'Because it was the son of my father.' It burned.

The young priest didn't move.

She looked at him.

'I don't know why I'm telling you all this.'

'You're telling it to God.'

'I'm telling it to you.'

# 11

The next morning the first to stop by the concierge's lodge was Viola, holding four wrapped pastries and jingling the bracelets at her wrist.

'Now I'm spoiling you, Pietro,' she said as she entered. '*Cornetti alla crema*.'

'I've already had breakfast, thank you.'

She put the packets down on a wicker chair.

'Everything all right?'

The concierge held out her post to her and checked a note that he had made in his diary.

'Nicolini the magician is coming to see the courtyard for the little girl's birthday.'

'I was going to tell you. Luca has to leave for the hospital soon. He'll talk to you about it when he comes down.'

Viola looked at the Bianchi leaning against the wall behind them. It had been sanded down. Beside it were two open tins of paint, one red and one bottle green. She bent down and picked up a brush, dipped it into the red.

'I'll just try.'

She painted a bit of the top tube and nodded to herself, painted another bit and blew on it.

'Now get on.'

Pietro kept his back to her.

'C'mon, it'll suit you. Get on. Without getting wet paint on yourself.'

The concierge hid his hands in his pockets. The sandpaper had abraded his palms and cut up his thumbs. When he had come down from the roof terrace he had begun to strip the Bianchi, in a fury. The front fork came first and then everything followed. He had stopped when the doctor had returned from the hospital, in the dead of night.

'It was just to see how you looked on it.'

Pietro hesitated, then climbed on the Bianchi and grasped the handlebars.

Viola smiled, like in the photograph of the lavender field, full of candour and sensuality.

'It's official: red.' She slipped her post into the pocket of her jeans and rested a hand on his back.

'And you'll be sorry if you don't let me know when you've finished painting it. We'll have to have a test run.'

'Test run for what?' A voice came from the entrance hall.

Both of them turned around. Riccardo smiled at the lodge door. He was holding a backpack.

Viola tightened the straps on her shiny high heels, clicked them against each other. Gathered up the pastries, no longer looking at the concierge. 'I'll go and make coffee.'

The radiographer remained on the threshold. 'Wait for me. I've got something for Pietro and then I'll come with you.'

She left on her own.

Riccardo moved aside to let her pass and watched her out of the corner of his eye, then came all the way in.

'The Martinis have invited me to breakfast,' he said in a lowered voice and laid the backpack on the chair. A man of sharp angles, his thinness was belied by the slowness of his gestures. The tendons on his neck stood out and his eyes were bigger than they ought to have been. They sparkled in a face of rough edges.

Pietro went to the letterboxes, pushed in a letter that was sticking out. He turned.

Riccardo was standing immobile in the middle of the room.

'I know that you met Lorenzo . . .' He appeared lost in thought. 'You know, I did the ultrasound on his mother, an odd woman.' He opened the backpack and drew out a heavy chain as long as his leg. Then a padlock with the key in. 'Here, for your soon-to-be red Bianchi.'

'Thank you, but there's no need.'

'They steal everything in Milan.' Riccardo put down the chain and made to leave. 'I forgot, you haven't by any chance found a leather bracelet?'

'I haven't found anything, sorry.'

'I must have lost it playing football.' He went out.

The concierge waited for him to climb the stairs then went into his flat. Rummaged around in the night-table drawer. Drew out the bracelet he had found in the courtyard and looked closely at the date etched on the back: *14-9-2008*. Closed it in his fist.

When Nicolini the magician arrived, the Bianchi was in several pieces. Pietro had taken it apart and placed the frame on some old newspapers. He saw him enter as he was stirring the red paint in its tin.

'Why do you need to get a look at the courtyard?'

'Magic needs its own space.'

He accompanied him into the courtyard and as soon as Nicolini began to stroll about, the second floor began to empty. Viola came down with the little girl. Pietro did not greet her and returned to painting the Bianchi. It was the fifth time in forty years that he had shed its skin and given it a new one, and he had yet to learn how to do it properly. He painted in all directions and failed to remove the excess paint from the bristles. Rivulets ran together and clotted, studding the frame with pustules. He tried to burst them by rubbing a rag along the surface. His hands became spattered and he tossed the brush down. Fernando and his mother and the lawyer appeared immediately after. They greeted him, Poppi with a wink, and went out.

Martini came down with the radiographer when there remained just a tiny bit of painting to finish the Bianchi. As soon as he went to speak with the magician, Riccardo went over to Pietro.

'Faster. If the colour dries on you, you'll be able to see signs on the frame.'

'Do you want to do it?'

'I wouldn't dare.'

The concierge hastily finished the painting then moved newspapers and frame into the courtyard where a shred of sunshine shone. The magician approached him after Martini and the radiographer left.

'A perfect courtyard for spells.' He mimicked the flick of a wand. 'I'll be happy to set up the day before. I'll turn you all into toads.'

The concierge accompanied him to the street door. Nicolini made a half bow in farewell and left the building.

That was when Pietro saw Snow White. The woman who had let Dr Martini into the house of the pomegranates. She was standing transfixed in front of the intercom grid.

'Pardon me . . .' Snow White came toward him, her raven hair strangled by a red ribbon. 'Pardon me, does Dr Martini live here?' She was very young and had a foreign accent.

The concierge nodded.

'So the "Martini" on the intercom is him.' She brushed the hair from her forehead. Her cheeks showed signs of past acne. She continued to twist a lipless mouth, extended a hand to buzz.

'The doctor isn't home.' Pietro took a step toward her. 'Can I help you?'

The woman said no and dropped her hand, raised her eyes to the first-floor windows. She tapped the heels of her boots as if shivering, crossed the street and waited on the other side.

Pietro returned inside to the lodge, opened a cupboard and picked out a cloth and the multipurpose cleaner. Went back outside and began to polish the grid of intercom buzzer buttons. Made four passes from top to bottom and meanwhile watched Snow White out of the corner of his eye. After a while she crossed over again.

'Do you know when the doctor gets back?' She attempted a smile. 'He's not at the hospital, and it's urgent.'

'You can leave word with me.'

'He's not picking up his mobile.'

'You can leave word with me.'

Snow White turned in a circle.

'I'll write him a note.'

Pietro told her to follow him, led her inside to the lodge and closed the door. He offered her the back of an advertising flyer and a pen. The woman took a seat at the table. She was even prettier seated, holding one arm as if she had a child in her lap. When she finished writing she folded the sheet of paper four times.

'It's urgent.' She handed it to the concierge.

He immediately placed it in his pocket. 'I'll give it to him as soon as he returns.'

'Thank you.' Snow White left the lodge and continued outside.

Pietro hurried into his flat, peered out of the small window above his bed. The woman was nowhere to be seen. Then he pulled the paper from his pocket, opened and held it under the light, read *Come as soon as you can. It's important. Sofia.*

He held it in his palm as he took the 'Back soon' sign from the table drawer, planted the suction cup on the lodge window.

He went to look for the doctor.

# 12

He found Dr Martini on the ward, talking with two other physicians and consulting a medical file. Pietro made his presence known and waited for him in front of the bulletin board with the crayon drawings, all shapeless scribbles except an aeroplane with two crooked wings in a fiery red sky. It was signed in the corner, *Giulio*, every letter a different colour.

'He'll be a great pilot.'

Pietro turned around.

The doctor adjusted his coat.

'Giulio will be a great aerobatic pilot.' He pushed down on the tack holding the drawing. 'Two visits in two days, Pietro?'

'There's a message for you, Doctor.' He gave him the note from Snow White. 'She said it was urgent.'

Martini read it.

'When was she there?'

'Forty-five minutes ago.'

The doctor read the note again and appeared distracted, then noticed the gift-wrapped package that the concierge was holding at his side.

'Is that for Lorenzo?'

'I saw it in a shop window on my way here.' He came closer. 'The woman who wrote the note said it was urgent.'

Martini looked at him.

'Lorenzo will be happy to see you. Come.'

He followed him into the waiting room, which was

deserted. The smell of soup choked the air. Murmurs came from the patients' rooms. Pietro heard a rustling, a cry. They went down a narrow corridor and turned into the second room on the left. Weakly glowing overhead lights illuminated two beds. A young couple watched over the first, where a chubby child sat up on a pillow and played with two figures made out of Plasticine. The young woman said, 'I'm angry with him because he won't eat anything.' The doctor greeted her and passed on to the other bed, which was unmade and empty. On the wall above the headboard hung a poster of Donald Duck dressed as a pirate. Two wardrobes occupied the far wall.

'Do you see anyone here, Pietro?'

The concierge shook his head.

'Our Lorenzo is invisible today. He's doing it in protest because he wants to go to the lake. But I always know where he is . . .' He approached the left-hand wardrobe and opened it, discovering only clothes. 'Come on out now, where are you?'

Neither of them had seen Lorenzo watching them from the corner beside the other wardrobe. He blended in with the whiteness of the wall, genuinely invisible, with two fingers in his mouth and his pyjamas askew. Beside him on the night table was a silver-framed picture of him at the beach being hugged by a beautiful woman. Pietro saw the photograph first, then the child. He laid the gift on the bed.

Lorenzo slipped in and curled up under the covers.

'Did you see what Pietro brought you? Go ahead, open it.' The doctor turned toward the window and reread Snow White's message.

The child hesitated.

Pietro opened the gift, struggling somewhat to tear through the shiny paper with the blue bow as the little boy peeked out in curiosity. The concierge set aside the paper and pulled a rubber elephant from its packaging. It was the height of his palm, with short legs and a kind of carpet on its back. Lorenzo reached out a hand and seized it, plucked the carpet from its back, chewed on one of its feet.

The doctor refolded Snow White's message and stood in a daze before Lorenzo, not seeing him, not seeing either one of them. He awoke suddenly and turned around and began to gather clothes from the wardrobe. Went to the child and kissed him on the forehead, took him in his arms and told Pietro to follow them. They left the room ahead of the concierge, crossed the corridor and entered an empty room. 'Wait for me in the lobby, Pietro.' The doctor shut himself inside with the child.

The concierge did not have long to wait. Lorenzo emerged from the corridor almost immediately, bundled up in a blue down jacket that reached his knees, the shape of his tiny legs impossible to make out inside his jeans. He had a paper bag in one hand and the rubber elephant in the other.

The doctor took him in his arms and winked at a nurse, said to Pietro to come with them, then exited the ward, continued down the stairs and outside. He led them around the corner of the building. 'If you feel cold, tell me right away, OK, Loré?'

The child wasn't listening to him. The lake was there. Enormous, surrounded by bamboo as sharp as swords, with lily pads on the surface that made floating flowers. He'd seen them the summer he came to the hospital for the first time. With the cold weather the frogs stayed hidden, the water snakes too. Lorenzo wanted to get down. Swung the paper bag and swayed as he made his way to the shore. Sat down on a low wall and waited.

The doctor held his mobile and Snow White's message in one hand.

'I'm going to make a phone call, Pietro. Can you keep an eye on him?'

The concierge walked over to the child.

Lorenzo had sat the elephant down beside him and was looking at the lake. He inserted a hand into the bag. When he drew it out he held a handful of dry bread. He tossed it toward the shore, 'Ducks, ducks.'

Pietro looked for them. They swam at the left side of the lake, massed against the wall of bamboo stalks that surrounded a small inlet. The doctor emerged from behind them, his head and the mobile at his ear visible.

Lorenzo tossed more bread.

The ducks didn't come.

Pietro walked away. Came to the wall of bamboo, pulled up a small one and stirred the water. The ducks didn't move. He stirred some more, *C'mon, c'mon, to hell with you*. He leaned out further, *C'mon*. He flung the bamboo into the water and the ducks fluttered. *C'mon, damn you*. The flock broke up and some began to swim in the child's direction. Three of them, followed by some scruffy ducklings. Pietro remained in a low crouch. The doctor's voice was clear: 'I understand, I'm sorry . . . I'm sorry . . . not at home. I was clear. I'm not coming, let me be.'

On the other side Lorenzo had stood up on the wall and was launching arcs of bread confetti. He stretched toward the approaching birds. His face was nothing but eyes.

Pietro returned to the little boy and picked him up. A tiny pile of bones with fitful breath, he hardly weighed a thing. Pietro closed a hand over one of the child's hands. There was a scratch on the tiny thumb. He caressed it.

'Are you cold?'

Lorenzo shook his head, and continued to stare at the ducks fighting over the bread.

'Mama.'

Pietro continued to caress the small cut. Pinched the boy's nose and his hands became wet. Lifted them up, saw blood mixed with traces of the paint from the Bianchi. He bent over the child: two dark rivulets of blood issued from his nostrils. He called and gestured to the doctor to come right away, flailed his arms, called him again.

Martini hurried over. He pulled out a handkerchief and cleaned the boy's nose and mouth. 'Let's go back inside now, little man.'

'Mama.'

The doctor bent down and pulled him up. The quack-quack of the ducks rose from the water.

'That's right, he was my father's son.' The witch detached herself from the young priest and did up the last button of his nightshirt, crossed her legs. 'Papa always took advantage of me. Can God keep this secret?'

'God keeps all the secrets of the world.'

'He's got to tell them to somebody, if not . . .' the witch leapt up and tiptoed towards the far end of the church, came to the altar '. . . if not, he'll explode.'

The young priest walked towards the far end of the church as well, entered the sacristy. He soon returned with a wafer and half a glass of red wine.

The witch took the wafer and held it up against the light, ate the wafer and it stuck to her palate.

He gave her the wine.

'Herein lie the secrets of the world.'

The witch drank.

'So that's why it tastes like vinegar.'

# 13

Pietro sat down in the waiting room. The doctor soon emerged from Lorenzo's room, without his white coat and carrying a document case under his arm. Spoke intensely with another doctor and walked over to the concierge.

'I'm done. I'll give you a lift.'

'How is the boy?'

'Exhausted.' He shook his head. 'It's my fault. I wanted to take him to the lake before his mother came to pick him up. She's decided to have him cared for at home.'

Dr Martini descended the stairs. Pietro struggled to keep up. Then they froze in their tracks. The old man in the petrol-pump attendant's jacket and cap stood in the middle of the path. In the same place Pietro had seen him the previous evening, with the same ravaged face. He extended a hand. 'Doctor, I wanted . . .' He went up close. 'I wanted . . . please . . .'

Martini walked right past him.

The old man addressed Pietro. 'Tell him to listen to me, please, tell him . . .'

The concierge stared at him for a time, then followed the doctor down the underground-parking ramp to a dusty car, the rear windows covered with butterfly-shaped curtains.

Martini got in.

'He's a poor devil who doesn't know how to pass the time.' As he set off he noticed that on the dirty windscreen someone had written with a finger, *Wash me, please*. He pointed to the glass. 'It's Riccardo, he lets me know when I've exceeded the limits of decency.' He drove with the document case on his knees. In the back were Sara's car seat and a stuffed animal, facing away, with the words *Hello Kitty* on one sleeve, wrapped in a checked blanket.

'Have you known him long?'

'Riccardo? Yes, for a long time.' Martini drove two blocks before opening his mouth again. 'On the first day of school I found myself seated next to this curly-headed kid. "Pleased to meet you my name is Riccardo but you have to call me by my last name Lisi," he says to me. A real scrapper. They separated us after fifteen minutes because we wouldn't shut up. Same in middle school. Same in upper school.' He smiled and now his eyes were visible. They gleamed. 'At university it was medicine for both of us, and every lesson a cock-up. He stuck to me like a limpet.'

The concierge rested his hands one in the other, paint from the Bianchi still stuck to one thumb.

Martini slowed down.

'I was the only one he had left. He lost his parents when he was a boy. Now it's me, Viola, and Sara.'

In the middle of the boulevard a line of cars was forming. Just ahead a van was parking and blocking two lanes. They turned down a side street, circled the block and returned to the boulevard, entering ahead of the van. The doctor slipped his arms out of his coat, leaving it on his shoulders.

'I forgot to thank you. For the elephant.'

'I didn't know what to get for him.'

The doctor settled back on the seat.

'Lorenzo is partial to elephants.' He nodded. 'So am I. Ever since I read that they take care of the herd without regard to kinship.' He was driving slowly now. 'All for all. A kind of doctor of the savannah.'

'All for all.'

The doctor slowed down again, arrived first at a traffic light and looked lost in thought. Then said, 'I should try again.'

'What's that, Doctor?'

'Do you have something to do right now, Pietro?'

'No.'

Dr Martini veered in the direction opposite to home. The checked blanket slipped off the back seat and he reached back to pick it up.

'My mother made it for Sara. She was very handy with knitting needles.'

He put the checked blanket on the seat and added the document case. Skirted a piazza with a war memorial and continued along the road that led to the airport. Not much later he turned into a residential street, stopped before an art-nouveau villa with two olive trees in the front garden and putti decorating the balconies.

'This is Lorenzo's house, I won't be a minute.' Then he stared at the steering wheel without moving. 'Pietro . . .' he said, 'don't you miss your job as a priest?'

'One can tire of a job.'

The doctor got out and walked toward the villa. Pressed

the intercom button, pressed again and on the lower balcony appeared the woman Pietro had seen in the picture on Lorenzo's night table. Beautiful like she was in the photograph, with a powdered face and bright red lipstick, she tossed her cigarette and went back inside. She soon emerged into the front garden in bare feet. Remained on her side of the gate.

The concierge stretched out a hand to the stuffed animal, then to the blanket. The wool didn't itch. He created a nest from small bits of fluff while continuing to watch the beautiful woman facing the doctor. She held her small, porcelain-like hands to her chest. Began to scratch the back of one hand as the doctor spoke, switched to the other hand and dug more intensely, bowed her doll's head. Pietro brought the blanket to his nose: the past smelled of nothing. Replaced it carefully on the seat and picked up the document case, unzipped it. Inside were a piece of paper with the hospital logo showing the weekly shifts, a packet of sugarless chewing gum, two fountain pens and four keys on a cord. Also two smaller, identical keys. He held these in his palm, thought about the only locked drawer in the doctor's study. Put everything back and looked at the beautiful woman again. She was speaking vehemently and her porcelain hands had become livid. She hid them behind her back and the doctor returned to the car.

'Stubborn woman. She's really set on bringing him home.' Dr Martini started the car and released the hand brake, thumped a hand against the steering wheel and set off. Passed a car and turned onto the boulevard they had come from, abruptly pulled his foot off the accelerator. 'The person who gave you the note today . . .' He stared at Pietro. 'Did anyone else in the building see her?'

'I was the only one there.'

They stopped at a stop sign. The doctor faced his side window as he spoke. 'If she comes back, don't listen to her. Don't let her in. And the same goes for the old man that you saw earlier at the hospital. Understood?'

'Understood.'

'If they do show up again, please let me know.'

Pietro nodded, cleared his throat. 'Do you have anything to do right now, Doctor?'

'What do you mean?'

'Do you have anything to do right now?'

'No.'

'Will you come with me somewhere?'

# 14

Anita's shop was a cupboard ten feet square in the city centre. It was her, two lamps in the style of old English gas lights, two and a half rows of hand-sewn clothing. In Rimini people said that the T'massons' daughter, Anita, after her parents died, had made her fortune in Milan and never came back. *She's a seamstress for rich people now but she's still not married.*

Dr Martini parked almost directly opposite.

'What do you need to buy?'

'A scarf.'

'Let's get this scarf, then.'

Pietro had been at the shop in the four days prior to his becoming a concierge. He kept Anita company as she opened, leaving as soon as the first customer arrived. From the shop's neighbourhood, a sort of village restored by wealthy Milanese, he would push on as far as the Duomo, whose pallor and pigeons, if nothing else, recalled Rimini's cathedral, then stay to watch the people in the piazza and the lead sky that never turned blue. Only on the day before beginning the concierge job did he approach the condominium. He sat in the blue armchair at Alice's cafe and ordered a coffee, then waited. Caught a glimpse of the doctor almost immediately. Knew it was him from the photograph in the envelope with the Salgari stamp.

'Good afternoon.' The concierge led the way into the shop.

Anita was at the counter, with four pins in her mouth and a nude mannequin to be re-dressed.

'Look who's still alive after all . . .'

The doctor appeared behind Pietro.

She pulled the pins out of her mouth, smoothed down her jacket and came forward. A fabric flower was pinned to her lapel.

'Good afternoon.'

'May we take a look around?' Pietro removed his jacket.

'Of course.'

Dr Martini set to browsing, went up to the skirts, to the hats, glanced at the necklaces hanging from glass bottles. They were made of bamboo coral and amethysts, of gemstones and freshwater pearls.

'Please take them off the bottles if you like.'

The doctor lifted off the amethyst necklace and held it in his hand. The stone shone violet under the light. He replaced the necklace and walked over to where Pietro was searching through the shirts. He searched as well, chose one that was pastel red. It had a French collar and blue buttons except for the lowest one, which was grey.

'Nice,' he said and held it up to his chest. 'But I don't have the right character.'

Anita came over. 'And what is the right character?'

'Red requires a certain personality.'

She drew aside the changing-room curtain. 'Let's see this personality.' She motioned for him to enter.

The doctor shrugged his shoulders and obeyed. 'Perhaps she's sincere?'

'Pitiless,' Pietro said.

He closed the curtain behind him.

On the counter stood a platter of macaroons protected by a glass dome. Pietro raised it and ate the coffee-flavoured one. Beside the platter he saw the deck of tarot cards buried under balls of wool. 'How's it going with the shirt?'

'It fits perfectly.' Luca emerged from the changing room. The red lent courage to his bewildered face. He smoothed his hair down.

'Suits you to a T.' Anita threw open her heavy arms and turned to Pietro. 'And what do you think?'

The concierge swallowed the macaroon. 'To a T.'

'Viola will think I'm mad.'

'This Viola will think you're handsome.'

'You don't know my wife.'

Anita plucked at the flower pinned to her jacket. 'Blonde or brunette?'

'Blonde.'

'If you don't mind my asking . . . How did you meet her?'

The doctor smiled. 'From a window.'

'Our Juliet will go crazy for the shirt . . .' She fished out a pair of polka-dot gloves from a drawer. 'And our Romeo here will seduce her for the second time with these . . .' She held out the gloves. 'Polka dots will go perfectly with a wife like yours.'

'And how do you know this?'

She pronounced the word with effort: 'Instinct.'

The doctor returned to the fitting room. Pietro chose a scarf at random from a wicker basket. Anita went over and wrapped it around his throat, whispering, 'You look fine, fine, fine. Come and see me tonight.'

Luca re-emerged. 'You found your scarf.' He took it from him and headed for the register.

She went round to the other side of the counter. 'Man in red, woman in polka dots. For life.'

'Better than a session with an analyst.'

'Would you like a discount?'

'As well?'

Pietro drew out his wallet. The doctor told him not to even try it.

Anita placed the tarot cards before him. 'With your left hand, cut the deck wherever you wish. The card underneath will determine the discount.'

He looked at her. 'Seriously?' He cut the deck three-quarters of the way down.

She turned over the card underneath: 'The emperor.'

'Which means?'

'Forty per cent.'

The doctor smiled. 'You should be a fortune-teller.' He paid. She gave him his change and wrapped the polka-dot gloves in tissue paper and two lengths of ribbon. Then lifted the dome over the macaroons.

'Would you like a fortune-teller's counsel?'

He nodded.

'Give this Viola of yours a surprise. Take her the gloves right away.'

'The cards say this?'

'A woman says this.'

Dr Martini chose a cinnamon-flavoured macaroon. 'Goodbye.' As they went out he turned one last time to say goodbye, waving a hand like his daughter.

Anita waved back, and as soon as she was alone she laid out the cards for the doctor's future.

'Viola hates surprises.' The doctor laid the gloves on the dashboard. 'Which is a good reason to give her one. Do you feel like coming along?' He set the car in motion.

Pietro grabbed the inside roof handle. 'I do.'

Martini accelerated and pulled onto the ring road, humming a low song. 'That shop put me in a good mood. How did you find it?'

'I spent a lifetime dressing in black.'

The doctor laughed, passed under a triple-arch flyover and took the road towards the airport, stopped at a light. 'The woman working there reminded me of my mother.'

Pietro let go of the handle. 'Impertinent?'

'Prophetic.'

They travelled along a boulevard flanked by terraced houses and slowed down beside a tennis court. Just beyond stood a former factory turned fashionable events venue. They pulled over just short of it.

'Did you really meet your wife from a window, Doctor?'

Martini put a piece of chewing gum in his mouth. 'It was fifteen years ago. I was in my second year of medical school. One afternoon in March, Viola passed beneath my window. We'd known each other for a little while. She knew that I was with someone else but, because she's a headstrong woman, she also knew that a moment is enough . . .' He turned off the engine. 'And the moment happened when I came to the window to close the shutters. While she was looking up.'

'Good timing.'

'She'd already understood that we could do each other a world of good.' The doctor opened his door. 'She set me free, Pietro. Viola has a sense of dedication that brings you back to the world.' He smiled. 'Too bad she can't cook. Instead she organizes wonderfully tasteful exhibits, conferences, that kind of thing.' At the entrance to the former factory a group of people gathered in evening dress. The road was backed up with cars. 'And to think that she wanted to teach Greek.' Luca got out and began walking towards the crowd.

Pietro watched him disappear among the people then reached a hand back to the checked blanket and to the document case. He felt for the zip. When he lifted his head he saw the doctor returning. Pietro withdrew his hand.

'Too crowded.' Dr Martini got in and started the engine. 'The surprise is postponed till this evening.' He attempted a U-turn but took it wide and had to reverse. Backed the car into a side street where a petrol-blue SUV was parked with one wheel up on the kerb, its passenger-side door dented and scratched. They both recognized it. Both pretended not to have recognized it.

# 15

At dinnertime Pietro went into Alice's cafe. From the window he could see the second floor of the condominium. One of the windows with light in it was the Martinis'. After he and Luca had returned home, the doctor had gone to pick up his little girl from his parents-in-law's. The concierge had reassembled the Bianchi.

Now exhausted, he loosened his new scarf and collapsed into the blue armchair, eyelids fluttering. Soon his eyes closed completely. When he reopened them, Alice was serving his hot chocolate and staring at the image of Mastroianni hanging behind him. 'You look alike.'

Pietro pulled the cup toward him on the table. 'Thanks.'

'For the chocolate or for Mastroianni?' Her hair was pulled back, her brow furrowed with fatigue. She went to the counter and returned immediately with two butter biscuits: 'Actors get special treatment.'

Pietro drowned a biscuit in the chocolate, let it slip into his mouth as he drank. Finished with slow spoonfuls, his neck stretched forward for fear of drips. Gathered the last drop with the second biscuit then went to pay, a chocolate moustache above his lips. Alice pointed it out. He wiped it away with a finger and she pointed next to a small stain on his jacket.

'Dammit.' Pietro himself took the sponge from the sink and dabbed.

'Fernando hasn't come back.'

Pietro paid. 'He will.' Smiled goodbye and left. The cold whitened the street lamps. The concierge pulled his jacket closer around himself and crossed without looking. Hurried to the building door, began to struggle with the lock. The key was defective and would not turn properly. He strained and forced it a bit. He tried again and cursed.

'If you want, we can use mine . . .'

He turned. Viola was behind him, breathing heavily. 'Riccardo gave me a ride. He plays football near where I work.'

He looked at her, confused.

'Didn't you just see us in the street outside the cafe?'

Pietro said no. They went in. The Bianchi leaned against the concierge's lodge and smelled of paint. The chain and padlock were not in use.

'You painted the handlebars, even.' Viola touched the seat and pulled one of the brake levers. 'It could use a nice bell.' She held her purse against her stomach and picked at the clasp with a fingernail. Her face was troubled, her mouth darkened by traces of lipstick. 'Just a little spin now, a dress rehearsal for your favourite resident?'

Pietro stayed put. She hesitated, twisted the purse in her hands one last time, dropped them to her sides and said goodnight. Started up the stairs, the clicking of her heels slow and laboured, entered her flat. Once the concierge could no longer hear her he followed. When he reached the second floor the lights were already out. He approached the Martinis' door, failed to hear a thing. Remained there another moment then made to go down. Poppi's door opened. 'Are you looking for me, Pietro?'

'No.'

'My peephole is worth a thousand of those South American concierges they hire on the outskirts of the city. Thefts have gone up thirteen per cent, and then you know what day it is today?'

'Friday.'

'Even the walls know that on Fridays Fernando goes with his mother to sleep at his grandparents'. And until just recently the Martinis weren't home. This lawyer is watchful.' He had on a silk dressing gown and his usual slippers. He smoked from a cigarette holder and with one foot attempted to block the cat in. 'I note with pleasure that we're dressed up tonight as well.' He looked him up and down. 'Classy scarf. For the same bird, or have we increased the flock?'

'The same.'

'You put up with my nosiness. It's just to know what you're making of this new life.' He came forward. 'Satisfy my curiosity on one serious point, though. Do you still pray?'

'And you?'

'I never have. But sometimes I try to cover all the bases: a paternoster with a gin and tonic.' The cat escaped and bounded toward the concierge, who huddled in the corner.

'I didn't know they bothered you.'

'I'm allergic.'

'On a Friday night a pussycat's not enough. Come have a nip at my place.' He was careful not to lose the ash from the end of his cigarette. 'I'll shut Theo Morbidelli and all my curiosity up in another room.' The ash fell anyway. 'I entreat you.'

A burst of laughter came from the Martinis' flat. It was the doctor. The lawyer perked up an ear. 'Now playing: evidence of conjugal bliss. Is it really our Martinis?' He gestured for him to enter. 'Just a nip and I'll leave you to your carnal education.'

Pietro waited at the entry. The lawyer retrieved Theo Morbidelli and put him in a room, the cigarette holder on the edge of a wooden chest. 'Please come in.'

The flat was cosy, welcoming, and poorly ventilated, with a fuggy stench that took your breath away. Poppi grabbed a small bottle of perfume off a shelf and pumped. Piles of books inundated the two couches and a zebra skin served as a rug. The table was glazed, the chairs were glazed, and on the wall hung an abstract painting with a glazed frame. Bouquets of fake flowers sprang from several vases. A thick layer of dust covered everything. Below the window stood a rickety contraption with a gramophone on it. The lawyer ran a finger over the apparatus and went into the kitchen, a small room divided from the sitting room by an exposed-brick arch. He picked up glasses and the bottle of Scotch and told Pietro to choose one of the two armchairs beneath a giant poster of Maria Callas that hung on the wall shared with the Martinis' flat. Surrounding Callas, Poppi had nailed up tribal masks.

The voice of Viola came through the wall as if she were there. *But the shirt looks good on you, you know? This red really knows its business.*

The lawyer clasped Pietro's wrist with all ten of his fingers, which were ice-cold. 'Sit down, my friend.' He sat down first himself and pointed to a yellowed arc on the surface of the wall. Leaned his cheek against the wall and the arc coincided perfectly with the shape of his ear. 'Do you know what the extenuating circumstances for busybodies like us are?' He poured the drinks. 'Loneliness. And forgetfulness. I listen out of emptiness, Pietro. I forget what I've heard out of respect. This is what separates me from the gossips.'

Through the wall he heard Luca laugh, saying, *Come here, my love.*

*I'm exhausted from work, unlike you who goes around buying yourself pastel red shirts.* They laughed.

The voice of the doctor continued, saying, *This is for you.*

*What is it, Luca?*

*Open it.*

'I love it when he acts like that. Somewhere between romantic and virile, a Robespierre of the emotions.' The lawyer handed him a glass.

Pietro drank.

Poppi drank as well, swept away three cat hairs from the table. 'Pardon the mess. Daniele used to take care of the house.' Swept away another two hairs. 'He was the one who cleaned.'

'For how long?'

'For twenty years. Then he died of a heart attack.' From the shelf he drew down matches and the stump of a scented candle, which he lit. 'And just think: I was never unfaithful to him.'

'You held out for twenty years?'

'Thanks to them, yes.' He lightly tapped the wall, leaned an elbow on the table between their chairs and his chin on his hand. Let his head incline, his ear touch the wall.

*But these gloves are gorgeous, where did you get them?*

The lawyer shifted the candle to the middle of the table. It gave off a nauseating odour. 'I've saved myself for them.'

Pietro poured himself another drink. 'I understand.'

'I know.'

'You know?'

'I've known since I first interviewed you for the job.'

'What do you know?'

Poppi stretched out his arm to the wall and lifted off one of the tribal masks. 'I knew that being dropped by God wasn't something a dating service could fix. And that concierge work is a good antidote for emptiness.'

'It was I who dropped God.'

'Then Our Lord must really have done you wrong. Did he cheat on you?'

The concierge smiled. 'For a lifetime.'

The lawyer put on the tribal mask, holding it pressed against his chin. 'With this on I'm less ashamed to mind their business.' The mask's large mouth smiled. The holes of the eyes shone. 'At first, I admit, I did it for the doctor. Then I also grew fond of *Madame* and the dear child. And of the despairs of marriage, *bien sûr*.' His voice was a murmur.

'The despairs of marriage.'

'Forgetfulness separates me from the gossips, Pietro.'

They heard a dull thud. *Take it easy, Luca, or you'll wake Sara.*

*How did work go today, Viola?* They heard clucks and smacks – kisses. *It went well, half Milan was there.* They heard another kiss. *Was Riccardo there as well? What kind of question is that, was Riccardo there or not?* He repeated the question. She laughed and said, *What's got into you this evening, come here and I'll take care of you.*

'It's my favourite scene.' Poppi sighed behind the mask. 'Luca seems so shy but he knows what he's doing in bed.' Poppi was the mask. With his cavernous ears he listened to the doctor saying, *You and Sara are everything I have.* He listened to Viola: *Come here, Luca. Come.*

In the middle of the table the candle burned with a tall flame. Pietro lifted it up, held it over his other hand, tipped it and the wax ran onto his wrist. He waited for it to harden then rose and walked to the door. Before leaving he turned, one last time. The mask was bent over the table.

# 16

By the time Pietro reached his flat the lawyer's wax had dried completely, weighing on his wrist. He collapsed onto the bed. *You and the little girl are all I have.* He pulled his limbs in. *All I have.* The rice-paper envelope with Salgari was on the night table. In addition to a letter less than a page long it contained an old photograph of the doctor as a child during a school play, wearing a bow tie and a bowler high on the crown of his head. He stood apart on the stage, looking towards a group of children all older than him, all serious except for him. Luca was laughing slyly, with the air of someone who didn't give a damn about the play. Pietro caressed the irreverent expression, put away the photograph and dragged himself into the bathroom. Turned on the tap. The wax melted under the hot water. He avoided looking at himself in the mirror until he began to spread shaving cream from his neck to his eyes. They were weary eyes, not Mastroianni's. The razor passed from cheek to cheek and the cheeks shed their grey. He paid careful attention to the dimple on his chin, the crooked line of his mouth, the folds of his neck. When he was done he realized he had cut his cheek. The concierge rinsed his face, traced the nick with his little finger and continued up to his forehead, where a number of wrinkles cleaved the mostly smooth skin. He never touched his hair, which after sixty-five years parted itself. Pietro hastily dried himself, dressed in elegant clothes and passed into the lodge while tying the new scarf around his neck. The chain from Riccardo snaked around the leg of a chair, the padlock closed and with the key inside. Pietro turned on the lamp and directed it at a section of the table. With the pen Snow White had made grooves in the fake wood surface. *Come as soon as you can. It's important. Sofia.*

He wheeled the Bianchi out of the building. *Come as soon as you can.* No one saw him leave. Pietro released the brakes and set off down the cobbled street. The mist rose and the *chk-chk* of the Bianchi pulled alongside a tram, passed it and the tail of his jacket fluttered like a cape. He passed under one of the ancient city gates. Two men at the entrance to the Metro watched him rush by, saw sparks fly against the whiteness. Pietro held on to the slope of the handlebars. At the end of the descent the light changed to yellow and he accelerated, crouching down over the top tube. A taxi honked at the intersection, *chk-chk,* the gears slipped with the force of his pedalling, the Bianchi turned into a broad street with unlit street lamps. Darkness and fog were everywhere. He darted across the large square where they'd hung Mussolini upside down. The clock atop the mirrored glass tower showed a quarter to ten. He swung a leg over and continued on with both shoes on a single pedal, dismounted in front of the gate with the sign reading 'Walk bicycles and motorcycles.' The ink had run and the letters could hardly be made out.

Pietro pushed the intercom button. 'Anita, it's me.'

He left the Bianchi in a bike rack containing more abandoned wheels than frames. Took staircase B. The stink of fried food issued from the walls and accompanied him to the first floor. Anita was waiting for him at the door, brushing her hair to one side and speaking to a much younger woman. She had removed the jacket with the fabric flower and wore a long woollen dress. 'Pietro, here you are.'

'Sorry I'm late.'

'Did you have dinner?'

'I ate something.'

'I know your something. One day you'll starve to death.'

'Good evening,' he said to the young woman, who was applying lip gloss to a heart-shaped mouth. Responding with a nod of her chin then lowering her head, she wore a skirt that fell above the knee. Continuing to apply lip gloss, she said goodnight and went into the flat next door.

'Silvia is shy.' Anita set down the brush and smiled. Below her fleshy face a necklace of pendants jingled. 'Now tell me, what adorable individual sold you this fantastic scarf?' She gestured to him to enter, pulled the curtains closed. Her dress hid large hips. 'He's the most handsome doctor in Milan.'

Pietro tried and failed to suppress a smile. 'The shirt was a hit.'

'I wish I'd been there. And the gloves?'

'An even bigger hit.'

'This Viola is a connoisseur.' She kissed softly the cut he had given himself with the razor. 'He has your eyes. Your hands, too. And he's also awkward like you.'

'What does that mean?'

'That you're awkward.' She took his face between her fingertips. 'His mother must have had an amazing pair of lips. Do you have a photo of them together? I could use one.'

'For your tarot reading?'

She pulled a face. 'I need it. Please bring me one.'

'Anita. You read his fortune, didn't you?'

'In the thirty years I've known you, you've never been so shameless.' She caressed his neck. 'Maybe once during a sermon.' She disappeared into the other room, returned with a package wrapped in tissue paper and a sticking plaster. 'For you. Even though what I should be giving you is a mobile phone. Did you lose yours?'

Pietro turned away and began to unpack. 'Did you read his fortune, Anita?'

'His fortune was in the first card up: the emperor.' She unwrapped the plaster and laid it carefully over his cut. 'The emperor is his future.'

He tore the tissue paper to reveal a pair of pyjamas.

'It's a silk blend. I threw your old pair out.' She moved away. 'The doctor will have to fight. Emperors have always had to fight.'

'Once there were others who did it for them.'

'Precisely.' She clasped one of his little fingers and led him into the bedroom, turned on the light on his side and retreated to the bathroom. He waited in front of the dresser. The pile of books had grown by two since the previous week. She had also added an old wedding bouquet to the mirror frame.

'A bride threw it to me a long time ago, but it didn't work.' Anita had put on a shiny dressing gown, swayed gently and her slight breasts rubbed against the fabric. Sat down with her legs crossed as she had as a child, when she and her parents would seat themselves in a corner of the church and he was a priest tottering at the altar. Pietro had seen her grow up and she had seen the same happen to the little boy in black who, during confession, instead of guilt asked to hear little stories about people's families and never gave penance for sins. He and Anita had become friends that way, in the confessional and over all those years, then when she had gone to Milan to study to be a fashion designer they had stayed in touch. She and she alone had been permitted to read the letter on rice paper.

'Even if I had caught two bouquets, it wouldn't have worked.' She took his jacket, unbuttoned his shirt, undid his belt and trousers, asked him to sit down.

'I can do this myself.'

'I'm doing it.' She helped him put on the pyjama top. He saw to the bottoms.

Anita reached one of her hands down.

And Pietro stopped her.

So she pressed a cheek against one of his and remained there.

'He's a talented doctor,' the concierge said. 'You should see him with the children at the hospital.'

'You can tell.' She helped him to stand. 'C'mon, you're dead on your feet.' She pulled the covers down, stretched out on the right side of the bed and occupied half of a single pillow. The other half was Pietro's. He set his head down beside hers and pulled her into an embrace.

'When will you tell him?' she said.

The concierge closed his eyes.

'Tell him, Pietro.' Anita rocked him ever so gently, kissed him on the forehead. 'He's your son.'

# 17

The witch's mother prayed that morning as well. She remained kneeling in the church's last row and bent down after each appeal for forgiveness. The young priest saw her from the altar. She went up to him and said, 'May God bless you, Father.' Then she left the church.

Pietro too asked for forgiveness, for what he was about to do. He followed her to a terraced house near the station. The mother disappeared inside only to re-emerge with her daughter shortly after. The witch had a pillow in one hand and wore a straw hat large enough to cover her shoulders. Together they took the passageway beneath the station and the boulevard all the way to the sand, then the promenade to the beach in front of the Grand Hotel. The mother stopped under a green umbrella in the third row. The witch retraced her steps and went up to the young priest. 'It's a sin to follow someone.'

'I wasn't following anyone.'

'It's also a sin to lie. And you need to put some sun cream on.' She led him by the arm as far as the huts. 'Here.' She placed the pillow in a trough in the sand dunes and lay down, turning her face to the sun and closing her eyes. 'Come.' She indicated the free half of the pillow.

'I can't.'

'Come. God won't strike down a bride-to-be and her priest.'

He looked at her. The bathing suit barely covered her chest. 'You're marrying the boy I saw in church last year?'

'He's from Milan too. I'll be with him in four days.'

'Do you love him?' The young priest sat down against one of the huts and apologized.

The witch pulled him by the shirt, guided him to the pillow. She took his right hand and laid it against her flat stomach.

He felt the smooth skin, and the emptiness.

'The one I loved was in here.'

# 18

The next morning Pietro returned late to the condominium. The lawyer was standing in front of the concierge's lodge. 'An ugly spectacle last night.'

'What are you referring to?'

'About *una checca in maschera*, a masked fairy.' He held up a teetering stack of paper. 'Here, from the postman.'

Pietro checked the stack and noticed that the doctor's newspaper was missing. He frowned.

'Don't worry, Luca's already picked it up. He couldn't wait to get to the gym this morning. Last night wasn't a great night for him either.'

'That's not the impression I got.'

The lawyer peeled off his leather gloves. 'It happened after you left. It had been a while since I'd heard them like that, him and Madame.'

Pietro stiffened.

'At first they really went at it, then the eggs began to break. Crack, crack. Madame was crying. I nearly had a heart attack.'

'What happened?'

'Forgetfulness, Pietro. Remember?' The lawyer pressed the red button to the right of the street door and it clicked open. 'It seems like your own evening took an entirely different turn, to judge from the sticking plaster . . .' He lowered the brim of his fedora and dived into the street, leaving the door ajar.

Pietro touched his cheek where the cut burned. Pressed

the plaster down and went into the lodge and began to distribute the post. There was an envelope for Fernando from the supermarket where he worked and a subscription renewal for Paola's magazine. The Municipality of Milan had sent two invitations to Viola. Each of the owners had received a notice from the building's management company. He flipped through the remainder and before heading into his flat looked up.

Through the lodge window, framed by the open street door, he saw that the old man he had met in front of the hospital was across the street in his *Total* jacket, holding the matching cap in his hands. He stared up at the condominium, his face's pallor blending with the facade of the building behind him. Pietro went into the entrance hall to completely close the street door then into his flat to observe from his little window. The old man had moved to stand next to one of the cafe windows.

'Pietro? Are you there?'

Voices were calling him from the lodge.

'Pietro?'

He rushed into the lodge. Viola and her daughter were standing before the grid of pigeonholes. 'Has the post arrived?'

He gave her the two invitations from the municipality. Viola looked them over while the little girl softly sang a nursery rhyme and stamped her tiny feet one atop the other.

Pietro greeted her. 'A snail told me that it's almost your birthday. Was it telling the truth?'

Viola lifted her head. She wasn't wearing make-up. 'Let's go, Sara, or we'll be late.'

The child did not move.

'I said, we'll be late.' She tugged her daughter by the schoolbag, tugged her again toward the exit. 'Move!' She yanked at her.

Sara obeyed but did not take her eyes off Pietro, fluttering a hand goodbye as she went through the door. The concierge was late in reciprocating. He watched through the closing door as mother and daughter crossed the street and passed beside the old man, who had again come closer to the condominium, hesitating on the kerb.

Pietro went out to meet him.

The old man, cap in hand, scrutinized him. 'Good morning, good morning,' he said, without moving. 'You know Dr Martini, you know him, I saw you together at the hospital.' Veins stood out like scratches on his forehead. 'Is he home?'

And Pietro said, 'My son is not home.'

The old man bowed his bony head, then hid it beneath his hat. 'Ah, so you're his father . . . Tell him . . .' he mumbled. 'He's a very capable young man, your son. There aren't many like him. He helped my . . . Tell Luca that Mario Testi was here looking for him. My son is really talented as well, all you have to do is look at him and you know he is.' He worried at the collar of his jacket. 'Tell him that I'll wait here today, please.'

'He won't come today.'

The old man's face further wrinkled. 'Is he at the hospital? Because this morning he wasn't there.'

'What do you need?'

'I'll wait for him here.'

Pietro walked away. He went back inside the condominium and picked up the most worn-out cloth, wrung it out in the courtyard sink. The Madonna, her face blackened by the smog, poked through the ivy. What binds all fathers? He climbed up to clean the statue, decided against it. He left the cloth in the sink and hung the 'Back soon' sign on the lodge window. He went out into the street, back over to the old man and said, 'Your son is ill?'

The old man coughed, leaned back against the wall, and Pietro knew that it was powerlessness. Powerlessness in the face of a son's fate binds all fathers. 'Is he ill?'

'My son Andrea is like yours. They're two young men on the ball.' He rubbed his hands together as if underwater. His wedding band spun on his ring finger. 'With the ball at his feet, he's amazing. You've got to see how he dribbles. Has Luca ever told you about my Andrea's dribbling?' He nodded to himself. 'The doctor came to visit him twice and he understood just how good he is.' His breath was ragged. 'Andrea always asks for him now.'

'I'll tell him you stopped by.'

The old man straightened up. 'You would like my Andrea.' From his wallet he drew a newspaper cut-out, of a boy on a football pitch, a ball under his foot and his arms crossed. Beside him was the old man years before, more fleshed out, with a brown moustache and hair parted to one side. He wore a skinny tie and his shirtsleeves were rolled up. 'And I'm sure that Andrea would like to meet you too.'

'I'm not a doctor.'

The old man carefully refolded the newspaper cut-out, placed it between the two halves of his identity card, which he closed with a paper clip. He lifted his head. His small round eyes were red. 'Sons who are on the ball recognize fathers on the ball. And vice versa.' He stood with his hands down the sides of his loose-fitting jeans. 'Sofia told me that the doctor lived in a nice building.' He gestured at the condominium. 'What floor is he on?'

'Sofia is the woman who came by yesterday?'

The old man nodded and without warning grabbed his wrist. 'I bet my Andrea would like to know the doctor's father.' He looked at him. 'Please.' He set off alone, stopped after a few steps and waited.

The old man lived in Snow White's building, beside the railway. With the daylight one could see frost on the improvised garden plots. He pointed at the only one being cultivated: 'That one's ours.' There were an array of cabbages and the two fruitless pomegranate trees. He shook the front gate. 'The lock is broken.' He cursed continuously until he managed to open it.

The hair on Snow White's statue was patchy with peeling paint. Pietro briefly rested a hand on her head, then followed him in. They climbed the external staircase. Pietro turned toward the row of sycamores along the street, looking for the one that had hid him after he followed the doctor. It alone was bare. Fallen leaves blanketed the grass around the trunk.

They climbed the stairs to the third floor. The old man's door had neither a nameplate nor a peephole, just a doormat well worn in the middle.

'It's me.'

The entry was a modest diamond-tiled square. Beyond it could be seen a small room with a loveseat and a television set on an empty drinks trolley. The smell of roasting meat hung thickly in the air. The old man hung his cap and jacket on a hall stand that already held a housecoat and a motorcycle helmet. 'It's me,' he repeated and continued into the kitchen and sat down. The table barely fitted in the space and the chairs squeaked beneath foam-rubber cushions. He poured two glasses of wine. 'Please, sit down, make yourself at home.'

Pietro sat and the old man pushed a glass towards him. On a shelf above the table were the disassembled pieces of a stovetop percolator and a packet of biscuits held closed with a clothes peg. Also three dried pomegranates in a shallow bowl in the shape of a tortoise. 'Is your wife still alive?' said the old man.

Pietro jiggled the glass, drank the wine.

'It's hard without her.' The old man worried at the wedding band on his finger. 'At least we have the kids, and work. The petrol station on the next block over is mine, come and visit me when you have nothing to do.' He poured out more wine. 'Sofia,' he called, 'Sofia.'

Snow White appeared in the doorway, in her hand a half-open book. 'Good morning.'

'This gentleman is the doctor's father.'

'We've met,' said Pietro.

The old man drank down the rest of his glass. 'I'm staying, Sofia. You go ahead.'

The young woman stared at Pietro, smiled slightly. 'See you later.' She lifted the coat from the hall stand and went out.

'I bet my Andrea is in love with her. They've got a class of women in Eastern Europe we can only dream of here.' He stamped his foot as if crushing something. 'My Andrea used to have a foreign girlfriend, Swiss, I think. But all he thought about was football and his motorcycle, and one day she got fed up with it.' His persistent cough returned to smother his laughter. 'Come and meet him.'

The hallway was a tunnel ending in a blue bathroom. There was a mirror on the wall and a small stand holding a telephone. The smell of roasting meat faded as the drone of a television grew nearer. 'At this hour he's watching all the shows made for housewives. They put him in a good mood.' He stopped in a doorway immediately to the left of the bathroom. 'Andrea, the doctor's father has come to visit us. What do you say?' Waited. Then invited the concierge to enter.

The concierge stepped into the room. The old man's son was a head on a raised pillow, his mouth and eyes those of a mannequin. His body, short and almost non-existent, was submerged below a blanket, between two raised wooden sidewalls.

'This is Andrea.' The father went round to his other side, caressed a cheek. 'You're happy to meet the father of our Luca, isn't that right?' He pressed a button to raise up further the head of the bed.

The concierge remained where he was. Behind the bed stood some machines. From one came a small coiled tube that led under the blanket.

'Did you know that the doctor has a beautiful house? He

lives near here.' The old man slid a hand below the covers and murmured something. 'I'll take care of you now, don't you worry about it.'

The old man's son's eyes were open wide. The eyelids stayed up. It was his pupils that rose and fell. For a moment they watched the television, for another looked at the three posters of footballers that covered the wall. Pietro recognized Roberto Baggio. Beside the posters, on the eraser ledge of a whiteboard, stood a sheet of Bristol board covered with doodles.

'How about a little light, eh, Andrea?' The old man turned on a lamp and one could see the whole of his son's face. It was broad, its slack skin sinking toward the mouth. The coiled tube ended in his throat, pumping in air and drawing out breath. A rivulet of saliva issued from his lips. The old man wiped it away and said, 'Today my Andrea is a little angry, isn't that right? Come, Pietro, come and really get to know him.'

The son's pupils rose.

'Did you know that Andrea and I draw? This one on the Bristol we did together.' He then pulled a notebook from a shelf below the whiteboard that also held a slim handheld recorder and a radio. 'These ones, on the other hand, he did a few years ago.'

Pietro paged through the notebook, saw sketches of seagulls, black-and-white-panelled footballs. Another seagull, an airship. The figures were gracefully rendered. Next to a football done in watercolours he read, *Andrea*.

The old man fiddled under the covers while smiling at his son. 'I'm almost done. The doctor's father is used to it – who knows how many people he's seen being changed at the hospital.' He squeezed out a sponge in a basin beneath the bed. The concierge backed away and the father cleaned the son as he needed to be cleaned. 'The real chatterbox in the family was my wife. Now, she was someone who knew how to keep him company. I only know how to put a petrol tube in a tank. Isn't that right, son?' He pulled out the basin and a rolled-up nappy. 'But you and I are like the strikers on Italy's World Cup team, we're like Rossi and Altobelli against Germany.' He whistled. 'We take everyone by surprise.' He disappeared down the hallway.

Andrea's pupils were transfixed. The tube in his throat hissed.

Pietro placed a hand on the side of the bed. 'My name is Pietro.' He placed it on the blanket and on a corner of the young man's body, which was like spoiled meat. He placed it on his forehead.

Andrea's pupils rose.

The concierge looked closely at them, saw that they were quivering. 'My name is Pietro,' he repeated before leaving the room. His gorge rose. He choked back vomit and drew a breath. Wiped his brow. There were no noises in the flat, just the stink of roast meat. He found the old man in the kitchen, on the same chair, his wine glass full and his son's nappy in his lap. A wheeze escaped him. 'I'm glad you met, very glad . . .' He drew the wadded nappy more tightly closed. 'Please tell your son, please tell him to come and see us. Just one visit will do, my Andrea always told me so before he got like this. He'd say, "Just one visit, Papa."' The old man brayed like a donkey, wiped the snot from his nose and headed toward his son's room. He returned to Pietro with the handheld recorder in hand. He spun it between his fingers like a playing card then turned it on. The voice of Andrea drawled beneath the buzzing of the tape. The old man raised the volume.

'My name is Andrea Testi. I am thirty-four years old and I know how to dribble. You have to have strong ankles to dribble well, and I have strong ankles. But what really counts is your eye. Look straight at your opponent, straight at him. Then ankle, ball, ankle. I can dribble right past people. I want to do it again.'

The old man stopped the tape. Rewound it and extended the recorder to Pietro. 'Your son will understand. He wouldn't accept it from me, but your son will understand if you give it to him,' he insisted. 'Please.'

Pietro did not move to take it.

'My Andrea wants to dribble again.' His father continued to hold out his arm.

The concierge accepted the recorder, slipped it in his pocket. The old man said thank you, pulled himself up and went to the shelf. 'My wife and I arrived here a lifetime ago. The first thing I did was to plant two pomegranate trees.' He paused in front of the bowl shaped like a tortoise. 'They say they don't grow in Milan, but we got the first fruit from it the month Andrea was born.' Chose one of the pomegranates, its dry skin bruised and scratched, and held it out to him.

'It's what's left of the three of us.' He coughed and the nappy slid to the floor.

Pietro accepted the fruit into his chapped, scarred hands and headed toward the door. Before leaving he looked back once more on that weary father. Saw him kneeling on the floor.

# 19

The witch's mother was looking for her and when she saw her among the huts she said, 'What are you doing over here, Celeste?'

The young priest slipped from the pillow, getting sand in his hair. Struggled to his feet.

Her mother noticed him and said, 'May God bless you, Father, if you manage to set my daughter straight, because there are sins here as well as misfortune.' But he was already away, beyond the beach facilities and running across the space in front of the Grand Hotel, to the fountain with the four horses. He hurtled down the boulevard leading to the station and then through the piazza, arrived in church, *Punish me*, climbed to his room.

The priest's housekeeper asked him, 'Everything all right? Are you hungry?'

He took off his shoes. His feet were quivering. He knelt down, then began with his sides. Beat them, moved on to his back and carried on down to his legs, beat them. Bent forward, reached back for his feet, squeezed them in his fists.

# 20

Pietro left the house of the pomegranate trees and sought out his sycamore. Powerlessness in the face of a son's fate binds all fathers. He leaned his back against the trunk. They are distinguished by devotion. He looked at his hands holding the pomegranate. He himself had never been devoted to anyone. Clutched the fruit, which was hard but not heavy, scratched it with a fingernail. Pietro continued to scratch it the entire way back and when he returned home he left it on the night table. Drew the recorder from his pocket and pressed play. *My name is Andrea Testi. I am thirty-four years old and I know how to dribble.* Pressed stop and dialled the Martinis' number on the lodge phone. No one picked up. He called again. It rang and rang. He took the keys and went out into the entrance hall with a damp cloth.

The only noise was the street traffic. He started up the stairs and stopped at the second floor. From the lawyer's flat came the murmur of the television. He moved over to the Martinis' door, rang the doorbell and waited. Flung the cloth to the ground, rang some more, waited less.

Opened.

The house was in order. The hall stand held a raincoat, the books had been removed from the floor, the dolls had disappeared behind the chaise longue. He crossed the living room and peeked into the kitchen. The table was set with a bowl of cereal, two cups, and a half-full bottle of milk. He pressed the cap back on the bottle and placed it in the refrigerator, caressed the ultrasound of Sara on the refrigerator door. Moved on to the doctor's study. Opened the drawer with the photographs. For Anita, he took the one with the woman and the newborn. Slipped it into his shirt's breast pocket and stood to leave. Instead he remained still a moment, then opened the drawer that contained the diary. It was still there. He picked it up and flipped through it. Luca had written various notes. On that day's date: *Mama, give me the strength tonight as well.*

He reread it and put the diary away. Tried the final drawer but it was still locked. Looked for the leather medical bag. The desk was covered with papers, atop which stood the computer, together with a paperweight and a plate with an apple core and a knife. He looked on the small couch and below the study window, in the sitting room and again in the kitchen. In the bedroom the covers were rolled up into a ball. The polka-dot gloves hung like rags from a chair and the red shirt from a hanger on the handle of the wardrobe. Pietro did up the top button. *Suits you to a T*. Looked around. The leather bag wasn't there but the document case was, beside the night table. He grabbed it and undid the zip. The two keys were pressed between a packet of sugarless sweets and a prescription pad. He returned to the study.

The first key worked. The final drawer rolled open and Pietro saw that it contained a bundle of five glass vials of a transparent liquid. On one he read the name of a medicine. Behind them he found a tourniquet, a stethoscope, gauze, a packet of syringes. At the back of the drawer there was more:

notes held together with a paperclip. He opened one. *To the love of my life, who if it wasn't for me would still be at the window. Viola.* It was dated four years earlier. He opened another. *I adore you when you say you want to have a child with me. Meanwhile let me love you. Viola.* This date was even older. He rummaged further and noticed a rice-paper envelope, identical to his but with no stamp. Torn open, its corners were crisp. He turned it over in his hands. *My son,* written slantwise. He drew out the contents, did not read immediately, stared at the writing.

*Luca,*

*When you find this letter I will no longer be. I'm about to die and if I'm not afraid, I owe it to you. Asking you to help me was the most difficult thing I've ever done. You said yes out of love. Now I'm ready. Who knows if God is beautiful like they show him to be. For me he doesn't have a beard and he lost his white hair a long time ago. Will he be as good as all that? Let's hope so. Be patient with me, I'm still a curious little girl. I'll go when you decide but I'll always be with you. Please be happy.*

*Mama*

He closed the envelope. Struggling to replace it at the back of the drawer, he touched something else, understood what it was and once again felt cold. It was a crucifix, the Christ figure smooth and without a crown of thorns. He grasped it and the top of the cross sliced his finger.

# 21

He gently closed the Martinis' door behind him and heard a clamour coming from the courtyard. He looked out from the window on the landing. Fernando was a bouquet of flowers and Paola a lilac trouser suit giving chase. The strange boy in his beret held the roses to his chest, protecting them as he skipped away from his mother.

The concierge waited. The cold in his bones was even colder. He picked up the cloth and descended the stairs. Found the lawyer at the entrance to the courtyard. He was wrapped in a trench coat and held a hand to his forehead. 'I've never seen such vulgarity.'

Pietro greeted him.

'The roses, I mean. No one gives roses any more. And the upsetting thing is that our Fernando is about to give them to her.'

'To Alice?'

'My God, yes.' Poppi turned around. His freshly tanned head gleamed. 'His mother just bought them for him. In other words, she's as good as sending her son to the slaughter. I tried to dissuade her but I could have used a right-hand man like you, my friend.'

'I was working on the stairs.' He tossed the cloth in a corner.

'You really have a thing for those stairs.' Poppi crossed into the courtyard. 'What have you two decided to do with those roses? I would put them in a vase at home and call it done.'

'We're on our way to give them to her now.' Paola took her son under the arm. Fernando raised the flowers and greeted Pietro. 'Today I'm getting married to Alice,' he said on his way out.

They crossed the street together, Fernando waving the bouquet to stop the cars. The cafe was crowded with people at the counter. The tables and armchairs were empty. They chose the corner close to the photograph of Sophia Loren in *Two Women* and sat down. Fernando was champing at the bit but the lawyer held him back. 'It's not with flowers that one seduces women.'

'With flowers,' repeated the strange boy.

'You just have to be nice,' said Paola. 'You've got your father's charm.'

'Of course, that's all there is to it.' The lawyer turned to the concierge. 'Do you have a plan for the imminent catastrophe?'

Pietro sat apart from the others, wedged into a corner of the couch. The cold had become ice. He took the bouquet of roses from Fernando's hands. The wrapping paper was wrinkled. He smoothed it out. Then stared at Alice behind the counter as she prepared two espressos.

Fernando stood up.

Poppi tried to hold him back.

The manchild gripped the bouquet, tipped his beret and started off. Cleared the tables and marched to the other end of the cafe. 'Alice.' he called out.

Alice had his back to him as she tidied the bottles of

liqueur. She wore a silver-coloured hairband and pearl earrings.

'Here we go.' The lawyer covered his face and peeked through his fingers.

Fernando swayed in his loafers, held out the bouquet and kept it suspended over the counter. 'Alice.'

She turned. Her gaze sought the back of the cafe. Pietro nodded. Everyone instantly went quiet.

Alice accepted the flowers. Fernando planted his elbows on the counter and waited for something that would not arrive. Waited some more, his face reddening, his heavy thighs straining against his trousers.

The young woman thanked him repeatedly, placed the roses atop the refrigerator and returned to the liqueurs. Fernando didn't move. Mumbled something, bounced up and down as if he were about to leap across the counter, growled.

'I'll go and get him,' said his mother.

'Let me,' said the lawyer.

Poppi went. He approached the strange boy, who wouldn't hear of moving, spoke to him and slowly but surely convinced him to leave the counter. Fernando ran to his mother.

'Come here, my baby. You just want your mama.' Paola made room for him at her table and kissed him on the cheek.

The boy wasn't listening to her but just stared at the floor, *Alice*, exhaling loudly from his nose, *Alice*.

'You just want your mama,' Paola repeated.

Fernando left her there, darting to the couch and curling up beside Pietro's flank. He was shuddering, his hands rigid like talons, his hat askew and hanging down over his face. The concierge stroked his back, stroked him again and placed an arm around his shoulders, slowly. Leaned into him, brushed his cheek with a hand and lifted the beret. Lifted it carefully and before the incredulous eyes of Poppi settled it down as it should be. Then he grasped three fingers. They were still talons. He stroked them and a little at a time he closed them. Reopened them and showed him how he must hold them in order to make the shadow of a parrot under the light in his beloved's cafe.

# 22

Pietro collapsed into the sunken middle of his mattress and slept for the entire afternoon. That evening when they knocked, he didn't hear it immediately. They knocked again.

He woke and pulled himself up. 'Who is it?'

There was no reply.

Pietro slid the door open. A coal-black eye came through the gap.

'Sara.'

The doctor's daughter was tightly wrapped in her little coat and had her hair loose. She smiled, a finger in her mouth.

'Wait a moment.' The concierge slid the door closed again and put on a jumper over his tracksuit. He stepped into his slippers. One of his big toes stuck out through a hole. He opened.

The child came forward. Held one closed hand behind her back and peered around inside, pointed at the two plants near the refrigerator. Pietro made way. 'It's a tiny, tiny house, for one person.'

She rushed in and circled the table and leaned on the wicker chair, all without saying anything. Continued to hide her closed hand, then all at once opened and showed it to him. Inside was a half-melted piece of chocolate with a card stuck to it.

'For me?'

The child handed it to him and bent down, touched the

big toe emerging from the hole in his slipper. She laughed, Pietro laughed too, then he unwrapped the chocolate. It had golden foil and contained tiny pieces of hazelnut. He popped the entire piece into his mouth and opened the card. Read the doctor's handwriting aloud: '*Mr Pietro, you are invited to my birthday the day after tomorrow. Will you come?*' He looked up. 'Of course I'll come. Thank you.'

But she was already across the room, seated on the edge of the mattress. She bounced in place, slid down into the sunken middle. Glanced at the night table. The rice-paper envelope lay below the pomegranate.

'I'll take you home, come on.' Pietro attempted to catch her but she squirmed away and first stuck her head into the bathroom, then hopped toward the bedroom.

He beat her there and closed the door. 'I will most certainly come to your birthday – with a lovely gift.'

The child tried to enter the bedroom.

'With a lovely gift.' Pietro picked her up and carried her into the kitchen, set her on her feet on the table.

She stood and looked at him from up there. Began to smooth down his hair, tugging a lock at his crown then pressing it down, one after another, then descending to the comb-over he'd worn for a lifetime. As she tried to brush his hair he held her hips. She was a Viola-faced munchkin. He pressed the child to his chest and she squeaked.

'Pardon me . . .' From the doorway emerged the doctor's top half. 'Sara, I got fed up with waiting for you.' He came in. 'Please excuse the invasion, Pietro. But with her it's always like this, she entertains herself.'

'Now I'm an officially invited guest to her birthday.'

'Now you have no way out.'

The child leaned in the direction of the closed room. 'He's got a chamber of secrets,' she said. Her voice was a murmur.

'A chamber of secrets, that's all we need.' The doctor went to his daughter and she began to brush her father's hair as well. Then back to Pietro's. And then the doctor's.

'Mama's waiting for you.'

Sara had herself lowered down and waved a hand goodbye.

'Bye, honey.' The doctor gave her a kiss, and when she had left, watched to see that she went up the stairs. 'She's been obsessed with that invitation all day today.'

'She's a quiet child.'

'And a very curious one.' Luca adjusted the raincoat over his shoulder, held his medical bag with two fingers. Put the bag on a chair, opened it and withdrew a bunch of five crumpled daisies. 'They were for Viola, but I didn't give them to her.' Placed them in an empty jug. His face was wan, mottled with shadow. He peered around like his daughter. 'Do you sleep there?' He pointed at the bed in the living area.

'I like cubbyholes.'

'And secret chambers.'

'Every priest has one.' Pietro went to the night table, pulled out the handheld recorder he'd received from the old man. When he turned back to Luca he saw that the doctor had sat down and that below the daisies lay loose petals. 'Night shift?'

'In your secret room, do you keep the sins of others?'

'How's that?'

The doctor plucked a petal. 'In your secret room . . .' Plucked another. 'Do you keep the sins you heard as a priest?'

'The sins of others are to be forgotten.' The concierge filled two glasses of wine. 'I keep my own in there.'

Luca drank immediately. 'I should have a secret room of my own, then.' He looked Pietro directly in the face. 'Nice and big.' Pietro looked back. The doctor struggled to keep his eyes open.

Pietro placed the recorder on the table and slid it toward the doctor. 'The old man in the petrol-station uniform came by.'

The doctor tugged at two petals simultaneously. 'I asked you not to listen to him.'

'He waited at my door. And he wasn't going away.'

'I asked you not to listen to him!' he shouted in a voice not his own. It was a frightening rasp. He poked a finger at the side with the microphone. The recorder spun like a top. He prodded it again, pressed play. The voice began and he turned off the recorder immediately. He bowed his head and held it between his hands. 'Did you listen to the tape?'

'I listened to it.'

'Did he take you to his house?'

The concierge nodded. 'Yes, I met his son.'

Luca lifted his face. 'Andrea . . .' One of his hands returned to the daisies and began to climb the stems. When he arrived at the flowers, he plucked. Plucked the petals one by one. 'The sins of others are to be forgotten, isn't that what you said?' One daisy stripped, he moved on to another. Plucked some more. 'It's our own sins that we keep.' Nothing but the stem remained. He moved on to another flower. When he finished there were five bare stems. 'I'm afraid.'

The petals curled on the table.

Pietro stared at him. 'I know.'

'No, you don't know.'

The concierge stood up.

The doctor said, 'I have to go.' But didn't move.

Pietro moved closer and Luca covered his face. The concierge removed the doctor's hands and replaced them with his own. Luca straightened his neck, from his mouth came the hoarse squawk of a crow, he drew a breath. 'It's not the hospital I'm expected at tonight, not the hospital.'

Pietro sat down.

The doctor looked him in the face. 'I won't make it tonight.'

Pietro held him.

That night the young priest got into bed as the *choooo* of the lighthouse blew. He ran a hand through his hair. The sand was gone. The witch's face was not.

He turned to the other side of the bed and slipped from the sheets. Dressed feverishly, *Forgive me, Lord,* opened the street door and ran through the piazza, *choooo,* ran down the boulevard to the station, took the street leading to the witch's house. As he approached, he saw that all the windows were dark except for one at the rear. The light struck the ceiling, where he saw the shadow of an enchanting profile, recognized the hair tied back. Beside the profile emerged two hands, intertwining. The shadow of the hands became a dog with its jaw open, a parrot with a raised crest.

He took a handful of pebbles from the ground and launched them against the glass.

The parrot dissolved and the witch opened the window. She stared down at him. 'You put on your nice shirt.'

The young priest stood with his arms at his sides.

Their punishment began there, with her finger held up to say, wait.

The doctor asked to use the bathroom. He splashed water on his face while Pietro hid the rice-paper envelope in the night-table drawer. When Luca returned his eyes were puffy and fixed on the closed bedroom door. He immediately started off, only noticing just before going out that Pietro had put on his jacket. Slowed to wave goodbye. The concierge did not return the gesture but simply followed him. They passed through the entrance hall, Luca in front, the old man's recorder swelling a pocket, his medical bag inclining him to one side, Pietro's shadow close on his heels. In the street Luca walked as if he were alone, only occasionally turning to see if the concierge was there. They travelled the street that passes under the ancient city gate, continued in the direction opposite that of the hospital. Pietro was a step behind, pulling up to the doctor at busy intersections. They didn't look at each other and each set off again on his own. They walked the length of Corso Vittorio Emanuele II and arrived at the cathedral, ivory under the extinguished sunset. They skirted the Piazza del Duomo, continued down a cobblestone street that ended in a six-way intersection. The doctor took the street that circled the Castello. Approached a stately building with a recently renovated facade, Pietro still holding back. The doctor buzzed and the street door opened immediately. Above them two stone eagles perched on the lowest balcony's balustrade. A little old woman stood behind the one with the beak worn away. Scrutinized them.

Luca paused for a moment on the threshold before entering. Left the door open a crack.

Pietro followed him.

The internal courtyard had a diamond-shaped flower bed with a palm tree at its centre that appeared ready to snap in two. There were two bicycles against one wall and in a corner a small fountain surrounded by a low wall of azulejo tiles. The concierge sat down on the fountain wall. A single drop spilled over from the fountain's upper basin into the larger, already full one below. A second drop spilled. The doctor passed through a glass-paned door and climbed red-carpeted stairs. On the first floor, two windows lit up.

# 23

Twenty minutes later the doctor came down, walked past the concierge and leaned his back against the inside surface of the street door. The leather bag swung from his index finger. Pietro hadn't moved from the azulejo fountain, now went to Luca and lifted the bag from his hands. On the first floor, the two windows had gone dark. The concierge accompanied the doctor into the street, back through the Piazza del Duomo, the polychrome Madonnina statue atop the cathedral defying the blackened sky. They returned up the Corso one behind the other, not stopping until the hospital. When they arrived, the accident and emergency department sign was lit.

'I want to say goodbye to Lorenzo. Starting tomorrow he'll be cared for at home.' The doctor took back his bag and lifted up his face, all sharp angles. Stepped towards Pietro but did not face or look at him. 'The woman on the balcony is the wife. He was my teacher in secondary school. He has intestinal cancer. He's tired.' Luca straightened his raincoat. 'His wife asked me who you were.'

Pietro buttoned his jacket. 'Who am I?'

'You're the priest who'll be confessing him tomorrow.'

'I'm not a priest any more.'

'You will be tomorrow.' The doctor stared blankly at the emergency department sign. 'Because tomorrow I'll be helping him to die.' He looked now at the concierge and truly saw him for the first time. Pietro was a tiny man whom the evening was nevertheless incapable of covering. Luca sought him with fearful eyes, then closed them. Together they walked through the hospital's front gate. They arrived at the entrance to the ward.

'Are you coming in?' the doctor asked, heading off without waiting for an answer. Pietro didn't move. He looked for something to support him, struggled to catch his breath, leaned against one of the fir trees. Then he raised his head. The windows glowed. He sought out a window on the first floor, confident he would see him, and he did. Lorenzo was there. Pietro drew a breath and waved with his hand hanging from his nose. The child pressed himself up against the window, hesitated. Then he returned the gesture, creating his own trunk.

Pietro headed back out to the street without entering the ward. He paused when he reached the pavement. An ambulance went past, its flashing lights staining him turquoise. When the lights were turned off, on the emergency department ramp, he started home. The concierge walked without haste, before his breathlessness forced him to stop altogether. *He needs me.* The effort choked him, choked him still after he arrived at the lodge and sat down in his kitchen. He felt for the drawer below the table and opened it without lowering his head. Felt some more, found a sack containing a scrap of bread. It was dry. He set it down on the table. Cut a slice thin enough to see through. Held it in the palm of his hand as he poured half a glass of wine from the bottle he had brought from the sea. With the bread and the wine he went into the bathroom. Standing before the mirror he saw what his tears looked like. Two rivulets trailed into his shirt collar. He lifted up the bread, broke it in two, lifted the glass and drank. The pasty mix swelled his cheeks. *He needs me*. He swallowed it down.

# 24

The witch opened the window and climbed out. Clung to the gutter. 'Be careful,' said the young priest. She began to descend. 'Witches fly, didn't you know?' He remained stock-still, hands stretched wide, ready to catch her.

She came down slowly. Her skirt lifted as she leapt and he saw two tapered legs, four sticking plasters on one knee.

'My mother doesn't want me to go out.' She took his arm, which was cold. Rubbed it warm and he could only grimace. Rubbed it more quickly and he laughed.

'Come on . . . Your name is Pietro, right?' She led him into the street, flitting noiselessly, a dragonfly dragging a horse. They flew to the Corso d'Augusto and the Tiberius Bridge, crossed it and continued down the gravel path to the park. There was a lamppost and a bench, four dark trees losing their leaves. He did not sit down but the witch did, and the leaves ceased to fall. 'Haven't you ever seen a pair of legs from Milan?' She raised her hands to the light of the lamppost. On the gravel appeared the blurry shadow of ten fingers. They closed into a fist and became a parrot. Then a dog, barking.

'It bites priests,' she said.

'Who taught you how to do that?'

'My father.' The witch stroked his fingers, spread them from palm to fingertips. They were uncommonly long, and made of iron. 'You can tell that you pray with these and nothing more.' She stroked the backs of his hands, drew them into light. And while he stared at her lips, on the ground appeared a species of crestless parrot. The witch tugged on his middle and ring fingers and the crest emerged.

'Move its beak,' she said.

He wiggled his thumb.

As the parrot's beak opened the young priest sought the witch's mouth.

That night, after he heard his son return from the hospital, Pietro started up the stairs and climbed slowly until he came to the iron door on the fifth floor. Opened it with some difficulty and went through. Walls of damp white sheets hung from the wires. He passed between two and felt the coolness on his face, arrived at the parapet. The narrow street was deserted, the sky a lightless pall. He continued to look up. *Will I go to his teacher's tomorrow?* he asked of the only father he had ever had in his life, the father who had remained cowardly silent throughout that same lifetime. The concierge slipped off his jacket, rolled up his shirtsleeves. Walked to the centre of the terrace, between the sheets once again, and stretched out his arms.

# 25

The next morning Pietro left the building with the Bianchi and pedalled slowly to Anita's shop. It was still closed. He waited in the saddle, leaning a shoulder against the wall and keeping his feet on the pedals.

'Pietro.' All of a sudden she stood before him.

He smiled and took the keys from her hands, helped her with the roller shutter.

'I was about to come to you, you scoundrel. You keep your mobile off, and . . .'

'I wanted to ask you something.' He kissed her on the head and ushered her in.

Anita had on a dress with a bow on the back. 'What happened?' She settled in behind the counter and turned on the shop's display lights. 'Tell me.'

Pietro laid a hand on the deck of cards, which was surrounded by balls of yarn. 'Shuffle.'

'You've never believed in it.'

'Please, shuffle.'

She laughed, restrained herself, laughed again. Watched him as she shuffled: he was a child, his eyes consumed with sleep and impatience. 'You've never believed in anything.' Anita held out the deck to him.

The concierge cut it in half.

She looked at the bottom card. 'You're challenging him.'

'Who?'

'God.'

She showed him the card, a woman forcing open the jaws of a lion. Uncovered for him too the middle card, a man on a throne. 'You're doing it for him.'

'The emperor.'

'Your son.' She spread the deck out on the counter, as far as the yarn. Exhaled noisily. 'Whatever it is you wanted to ask me . . .' Nibbled at a fingernail. 'The answer is no. Don't do it.'

'No?'

'The Lord doesn't forgive twice.'

Pietro did not listen to Anita's cards. For the rest of the morning he monitored the preparations for Sara's birthday. In the courtyard the magician Nicolini was directing the construction of a small stage. The lawyer stopped by the lodge around eleven with a brochure in hand and a haggard look. 'It's a disaster, my friend. It seems that Fernando won't ever set foot in the cafe again.'

'He'll get over it.'

'I hope so. Meanwhile . . .' He showed him the brochure, which showed two jockeys on horses. 'I've consoled myself with a gift for little Sara – riding lessons. The younger the better, in such cases.' He tittered. 'What did you come up with?'

Pietro bit his lip.

'If you forgot, you can always go in with me.' Poppi left the brochure with him and continued into the courtyard to inspect the operation. He stayed more than an hour, going back up to his flat only after the magician had gone.

Pietro set to sweeping the courtyard until he caught sight of the doctor coming down the stairs. Then he made sure he was in the entrance hall to greet him. Held open the street door and said, 'I'm coming with you.' Then, as on the previous evening, Pietro trailed Luca all the way to his former teacher's house. They stopped below the imposing balcony. The little old woman was there, wrapped up in a coat, her face greyer than the two stone eagles. She went back inside and Luca said, 'Why did you agree to come?'

'Why did you ask me to?'

'For my mother.' The doctor entered the building.

Pietro remained in the street, tried to clasp his hands together to stop them shaking, then crossed into the courtyard. More drops overflowed in the azulejo fountain. Beside it Luca, a stork swaying on the steps, waited for him. They went up together, stopping in front of a door with a brass nameplate reading *Morelli-Lai*. The door opened.

'Hello.'

The two-eagles woman welcomed them, bowing a chin covered with sparse down. She was a twig dried up by the years. The woman looked at Pietro, looked at the doctor. 'This way.' She indicated a room halfway down the hall. On the walls hung several lithographs and two Indian ink drawings of Milan in the last century. A stick of incense burned on a large wooden chest.

'This way.'

From the end of the hall came a series of coughs, ending in a rattling wheeze.

'My husband can change his mind, right?' she asked.

Luca kept his gaze on the stone eagle outside the French doors of the large sitting room. 'He can change his mind whenever he likes.' He laid his leather bag on a table and his coat over a chair.

'My husband is not a believer.' She turned toward Pietro. 'But I am.'

'I'll need the professor's signature.' Luca handed her a sheet of paper. 'I'll also need a glass.'

She read the document, left and returned with a glass, left the room once more with the paper. Luca pulled from his bag two glass vials, a tourniquet and a small bottle. Pietro stood next to a mantelpiece supporting a large bowl full of chocolates. Above it hung a shelf with a line of records from the 1970s (De André, Venditti, Dalla), beside it a small table with a book of poetry and a worn copy of the Gospels. The bookmark was a bus ticket.

Luca put on plastic gloves and poured two drops from the bottle into the glass. Looked at Pietro. 'It happened with my mother as well.' He drew out a syringe and a stethoscope.

The little old woman had meanwhile returned with the signed document and was now leaning against the door jamb. As soon as Luca nodded she led him to her husband. 'The doctor is here, Luigi,' she murmured as she entered.

Pietro saw his son enter the room at the end of the hall.

'*Moriturus te salutat*,' said a weary voice.

'Mr Morelli,' said Luca.

'The doctor said that you can change your mind whenever you want,' his wife insisted.

'The doctor was an excellent student with his head in the clouds. I remember him well.'

The woman went into the hall and from there into the bathroom.

'I promised her that we'd meet again, even if she's not very romantic these days.' The weary voice paused. '"But even as we press together tightly / and keep the crowding menace from our eyes / it maybe hides in you or hides in me/ because our spirits live by treachery". My wife agrees with the poet Rilke. She thinks that I'm betraying her. This time with death.' He coughed and spat into a basin beside the bed. 'I'm exhausted, doctor.'

'I have a friend of mine outside. Your wife told me that she would appreciate having a word with him.'

'My wife maintains that if I don't repent, we won't meet again. Death on demand separates the ignorant souls from the ungrateful ones, she says. I've always been ungrateful, so what difference would it make?'

Pietro was halfway to the room when the teacher said, 'Now tell me what I have to do, Luca.'

'Drink from the glass and set it back down on the nightstand. Nobody must touch it. Then I'll come.'

The little old woman came out of the bathroom, hugged the wall as she approached the room containing her husband, entered.

'Come here,' said the teacher.

Luca stood aside.

'Come here, my love.'

In the house of the two eagles could be heard her cry. She

squeaked like a tiny animal, *Don't do it,* her wail strangling her into an almost silent whimper. Abruptly the woman left the room and retreated as far as Pietro. He placed an arm around her and together they walked back to the sitting room. 'Tell me that we'll see each other again, Father.'

Pietro did not look at her.

'Tell me that we'll see each other again.'

The doctor joined them and bent over her. 'If you want, you can go and talk to him, ma'am. He has just drunk.'

'What did he drink?'

'Sedatives.'

The little old woman went and Luca took the two vials from the table. He shook them gently and filled the syringe, returned to the teacher's room while Pietro fished out a chocolate with a red foil wrapper from the bowl. Slipped it into his pocket and walked into the hall. Listened to the weary voice rise in pitch, the woman's break, 'I love you.'

The teacher inhaled noisily, breathed out with a wheeze, inhaled noisily again. There was an attack of coughing. Then the inhalations stopped, and in the house of the two eagles nothing more at all could be heard.

Luca emerged with the syringe pointed at the ground, didn't look at Pietro, disappeared into the sitting room. The concierge walked forward and came to the door at the end of the hall. Saw him. A skeleton with a recently shaved face. The woman held him in her short arms, rocked him side to side, and one of the man's legs slipped out of bed. The toenails were perfect.

'Bless him,' implored his wife. 'Bless him.' She continued to rock him.

Pietro dragged himself up to the old man with greenish skin and open eyes. He closed them.

'Bless him.'

And the priest did.

The young priest sought the witch's mouth and the shadow of the parrot dissolved. She pulled back and he murmured, 'Sorry, I don't know what I was doing.'

'You tried to kiss me.'

'I'm a priest.'

'You've got lips.'

'I'm a priest.'

'Who tap dances.'

He buried his feet in the gravel.

And she swung hers. 'They say that you didn't have any choice but to go with God.'

'They found me in front of a convent. I'm an orphan who's never had any other father.' He rubbed his lips. 'Where's yours?'

'Who knows.'

'Does the groom know about your son?'

The witch massaged her belly and shook her head. Then she took his hand and ran with him to the Tiberius Bridge. They stopped in front of a tavern with the roller shutter pulled halfway down. The witch knocked and a man came out with a broom in his hand.

'Do you have two chocolates?' she said.

'You blind? We're closed.'

'Do you have dark chocolate ones?'

The man shook his broom. 'A guy works all day, and at the end of the night he's gotta talk to crazy people.' He disappeared inside and immediately returned, handed her two chocolates.

The young priest's had red foil. She watched him chew and swallow.

'Do you want mine too?'

He nodded.

The witch unwrapped it for him and said, 'Your mouth is dirty.' She wiped a corner of his lips with her thumb. From across the street her mother's voice cried out.

## 26

The teacher's wife inclined her head goodbye as they left the villa. When they were outside they realized it was raining. The doctor pulled an umbrella out of his bag, and also the recorder belonging to the old man from the petrol station. 'I can't, not with him. Please give it back.' He moved off, stopped for a moment and said, 'Thank you.' Repeated, 'Thank you.' Then started down the street of horse-chestnut trees, soon becoming lost among the other umbrellas. Before opening his own, Pietro removed the chocolate from the red foil wrapper and placed it in his mouth. It was dark chocolate. The bitterness dried up his mouth as he turned toward home. He took a long time to complete the trip, and when he came to the condominium's street he turned in the opposite direction. Went towards the university and followed the railway all the way to the home of the old man in the petrol-pump attendant's uniform. Marched past the Snow White statue and the pomegranate trees dripping with rain. Continued down the main street until he reached the petrol station at the next junction. The station's plastic canopy struggled to cover the two cars in the queue. The old man, bent low, held a nozzle to the first car's tank. When he caught sight of Pietro he hurried over to him. 'Oh, what a surprise, what a surprise.' Wiped a hand on his trousers and extended it to the concierge. 'How are you, Pietro?'

The horn of the car being refuelled began to sound.

'They're in a hurry. Can you wait a moment? Meanwhile, make yourself comfortable inside.' He pointed to what looked like a metal shipping container with the word *Total* on it and ran to finish the job, whirled his long arms about the tank. Returned to him in a coughing fit. 'Forty years of cigarettes.' Covered his mouth. 'Please step inside, Pietro.'

Pietro did not step inside.

The old man entered alone. The container was furnished with two stools and a row of canisters of motor oil. 'Are you familiar with the story of the man who wants to stay outside at any cost?'

'I don't know it.'

He cleared his throat. 'There's this man who, ever since he was born, is terrified that something will fall on his head, so he lives as much as possible outside his house, outside his office, outside the cafe where his friends go. At most he stays half in and half out, like you right now. He doesn't care that his wife is about to leave him, his boss is about to fire him, and his friends make fun of him. He's happy because nothing can fall on his head.' The old man pulled a bottle from a cabinet, poured a splash of liquor in two plastic cups. 'One day there's a football match on TV and our man goes to watch it at the cafe as usual, that is, he stands outside the cafe because his friends arrange the TV so that he can see it through the window. That day it rains but he stays there with an umbrella over his head and his eyes fixed on the match. Then a lightning bolt comes and strikes him right in the head.' The old man choked back a laugh and drank the liquor. 'The lightning mows him down, understand? Gets him right in the head, can you imagine?' He handed the other cup to the concierge. 'Surely you don't want to get a lightning bolt in the head yourself?'

Pietro clutched the recorder in his pocket. Closed his umbrella and stepped inside. 'I spoke to my son.'

On the container wall hung an Inter Milan calendar. The old man rose unsteadily and stumbled into it. 'Oh, yes, tell me.' He began to cough with his hand over his mouth. When he pulled it away it was wet with saliva. The old man dropped it to his side. 'Your son listened to the tape of Andrea? Please, tell me.'

'You'll have to be patient.' Pietro left the recorder in his pocket. 'Sooner or later, he'll come.'

'Are you sure?' The old man went up to him, took hold of his arm. 'Are you sure?'

'You have to be patient, and leave him in peace.'

'Certainly, of course, we've got all the patience in the world. I don't know how to thank you and your son, all the patience in the world, I don't know how to thank you both.'

Pietro exited the container. Picked up his umbrella and before opening it looked up. The sky was empty of lightning.

The witch's mother cried out, 'Celeste!' She crossed the bridge and came towards her daughter.

'It's my fault.' The young priest took a step forward.

'You, Father, you stay away from this scourge.'

The witch scratched at her stomach and her ballerina's legs crossed. A tear fell from each eye.

Two tears fell from the mother's eyes as well.

His own eyes remained dry. They watched her move away en pointe, dragged by the person who had brought her into the world. She disappeared into the mist coming off the sea while the *choooo* of the lighthouse started up again.

# 27

During the night before the birthday party, Pietro woke from the nightmare that had been following him for a lifetime. Opened his eyes wide and saw, in place of the ship without a sea, the Bianchi glimmering in the flashes of lightning. The nightmare continued and a clap of thunder reached him. He waited for another. As soon as it came he wrapped himself in the bedspread and went to the two plants to the right of the refrigerator. Carried them outside and placed them with the others next to the stage that the magician had had built. Waited with them for the rain, bedspread over his shoulders.

The rain did not come. Fernando did. He appeared in a flash of lightning, wearing pyjamas and his beret. Huddled against the wall like a thief, he set off along it and stopped below the alcove containing the Madonna. Stood on tiptoe and attempted to grab hold of the statue. Failed, leapt, failed again. Knelt down and held his hands in prayer. When the sky flashed he covered his eyes and then pulled himself up. Dragged over a tower of stacked chairs, climbed on top and grabbed hold of the Madonna by the arms. He tottered and a whimper escaped his mouth. Tottered again and clutched wildly at the plaster veil.

Pietro was too late: the crack of thunder came and Fernando lost his balance. He and the statue landed on the boxes of decorations for the following day's party.

'Fernando . . .' Pietro rushed over to him. 'Fernando.'

The boy was motionless. Holding the Madonna to him and muttering, 'Mama is crying.' His glasses were twisted. 'Mama says that she doesn't laugh any more, she doesn't live any more. It's all your fault, because you're my son, your fault.'

Pietro helped him up. 'Come on.' He covered him with the bedspread and tried to lead him inside but Fernando wouldn't budge. They remained at the centre of the courtyard and the rain began to fall.

'Let's go, Fernando.' He raised the bedspread above their heads. He and the boy shivered and watched their feet lit up by the flashes, Pietro's terrycloth socks in holey slippers, Fernando's beach sandals. Between them the Madonna, her veil chipped and halo askew.

'Let's put her back,' said the concierge.

Fernando held on to her tight.

Pietro put his mouth to Fernando's ear. 'Ask her for what you want one last time, then let's put her back.'

The sky thundered. 'For Mama to laugh.'

The rain came at them diagonally, along with something else that wasn't rain. They were snail shells, falling from the ivy.

'Now let her go, Fernando.'

He didn't obey. 'You ask for what you want, too.'

The rain slowed.

'Ask her for what you want,' he repeated.

The bedspread was heavy with cold water. Pietro lowered it and they saw that fog had settled everywhere, swallowing them up. The concierge advanced with the statue in his hands and the snail shells under his feet, replaced it in the alcove. The ivy leaves shook in the wind. Rain streaked down the Madonna's black face.

He brought Fernando home. He had him sit down in the kitchen and told him to wait there. The strange boy's face was red and his beret soaking wet. When Pietro returned with a towel he found him gazing into the refrigerator.

'Are you hungry?'

Fernando straightened his glasses. 'I need to pee.'

'I'll take you back to your mother now.'

'I need to pee.'

He led him to the bathroom. Before entering, the boy stared at the Bianchi leaning against the wardrobe, beside the bed. 'It sleeps with you.' He pointed at the bicycle and went in.

Pietro went back to the kitchen. Put a pan of milk on to heat and took some stale biscuits from the pantry, placing them on the table. Then dried his head with the towel as the sound of rushing water came from the bathroom.

'All done, Fernando?'

He looked. The bathroom door was open, the bedroom door wide open. He rushed first to the bathroom. Water was running into the washbasin. Fernando was missing. The concierge turned off the taps and headed for the bedroom. The boy had switched on the lamp and was kneeling over the suitcase. 'Three, four,' he counted the boxes.

Pietro yanked him up, tried to lead him away. 'Let's go, it's late.'

'Are these your jewels?'

The concierge adjusted his pyjamas and replaced a sandal that had come off. 'Let's go.'

Fernando looked him up and down. 'You stole them from Dr Martini's flat.' Then he knelt again, ran a hand over the open boxes and made to pick something up. He touched the rusty bell, the notes, the envelopes, the red foil wrapper from the chocolate saved from that afternoon.

'I'm taking you home, Fernando.'

Then the boy made a fist and pulled out three fingers as he had learned at Alice's cafe. He moved them beneath the lamp. On the wall appeared the shadow of a blotch.

Pietro straightened the index finger and the blotch was transformed into a lopsided parrot. The manchild dissolved it and embraced Pietro with his bull's strength, then the smell of scalding milk reached them.

# 28

Pietro stayed shut up in his flat until early afternoon. The lawyer knocked and said, 'I just wanted to let you know that some brute is moving your plants because they don't figure in the birthday plans. Pietro, can you hear me?'

Pietro heard him, held a handkerchief to his runny nose and a pen to a crossword puzzle, one across: *word read from the left and from the right,* ten letters. The concierge didn't reply to the lawyer, as he hadn't responded to the decorators that morning who had wanted to ask him about the set-up. He had stayed in bed until he heard the doctor say to Viola, 'I'm going to go ask in the pastry shop. Make sure they arrange the chairs in herringbone rows.'

Pietro wrote *P* in the first square and sneezed, then went into the lodge. Through the gaps in the curtains he saw the first guest arrive. It was a chubby child who hesitated and came to a stop in the middle of the entrance hall, carrying a gift larger than he was and accompanied by two parents fresh from the tailor's. Viola was there. She crouched down and stroked his cheek. Had him put on a paper hat shaped like a cone. 'Go right on up to the second floor. My parents are there. I'll be up soon, then we'll come back down now that the sun is back, thank goodness.' Viola stood in a corner and as soon as the guests went up leaned against the wall. She wore a dark wrap and held the cluster of hats by their elastic bands. Let her arms fall to her sides, and the hats hit the floor.

Pietro went into his flat and pulled Riccardo's leather bracelet from the night-table drawer and returned to the entrance hall. He could see Nicolini the magician rehearsing on the stage, in front of the plants shoved to one corner. The concierge showed the bracelet to Viola. 'Do you know who might have lost this?' He sneezed.

Viola looked at him. 'Did you catch cold from riding your bike?'

'From the rain last night.'

She took one of the paper hats and offered it to Pietro. 'Are you coming to the birthday party? Sara is really counting on it.'

He returned to the bracelet. 'There's a date engraved on it: 14-9-2008. Do you know who might have lost it?'

She placed a hat on her own head, at an angle. It slid down over her eyes. She did not straighten it but stayed leaning against the wall with the cone of shiny paper covering her face. When she pulled it up her eyes were shining. As Viola settled the hat atop her head a tear dirty with mascara trickled down as far as her cheekbone. She wiped it away. 'Pardon me, it's just one of those days.' Then she took hold of the edge of his shirt. Pietro had seen her for the first time two days after his arrival at the condominium. The doctor's wife had introduced herself, taking his hand between her two. Had not said anything further, merely smiled. Paola had warned him that the doctor was in love with a flirt who only cared for herself and outfits that looked like gift wrap.

He removed her hat. 'Fernando and I have a surprise for Sara.'

Viola abruptly let go of the edge of Pietro's shirt and put her right arm behind her back. She looked intently over Pietro's shoulders.

The concierge turned.

The doctor was at the entrance. 'The treats are on their way, ten minutes . . .'

'Perfect.' Viola hurried up the stairs while in the courtyard the magician reached into his top hat and pulled out a walking stick topped with a silver knob.

Luca went over to Pietro, saw the bracelet in his hand.

The concierge held it out to him. 'Riccardo must have dropped it.'

'Let him come and get it.'

Pietro waited for the doctor to get inside his flat then went to find Fernando. There was no need to ring the bell. Paola stood in the doorway wearing shoes the colour of cyclamens. She was adjusting her silk scarf as she saw him. 'They've invited half the city.'

The concierge asked if he could come in. She motioned for him to wait and hastened to close the door that separated the living room from the bedrooms.

'Please come in,' she said, returning.

'I want to ask something of Fernando.'

'He's fallen ill. He's always sleeping without the covers on and last night he came down with a cold that I'd advise you to steer clear of.' She looked at his red nose. 'But perhaps you've fallen ill as well?'

From the Martinis' flat came the voices of the guests.

Pietro stepped further into the entryway, which smelled of rotting flowers. They arrived in the living room–kitchen. The room overflowed with knick-knacks and costume jewellery. A year-round nativity scene stood on artificial moss.

'Will you come to dinner one evening?' Paola took a few steps toward him. 'Fernando is so fond of you. He's changed since you came.'

'I'd like to speak to him now.'

'We've all changed a bit since you came.'

'I'd like to speak to him.'

Paola lowered her eyes and disappeared through the door to the bedrooms. The guests were beginning to go down into the courtyard. Pietro approached the small table where he had seen Fernando pray. The blankets were piled up on the couch.

She returned. 'He's resting. He'll join us later.' Hardly had she finished speaking when a tapping came at one of the glass-paned doors. Fernando pressed his face up against the glass. Paola went over to him. 'Go back to bed, you're worn out.'

'Not worn out.' Fernando opened the door and passed under his mother's arm. He greeted Pietro with eyes swollen from the cold, wearing a cardigan and loafers. He began to lead the concierge around the house. 'Choose one of my jewels.'

'Fernando, don't start,' Paola said.

The concierge bent over him. 'Do you remember Sara's gift?'

'Gift.'

'What gift?' Paola poked her head between them.

The boy stretched out his fingers, showed them to his mother.

'Pietro, tell me this doesn't have anything to do with that poor girl at the cafe.'

When they came out onto the landing Fernando raced down the stairs. Paola followed in pursuit. 'Cover yourself, you're ill!'

Pietro stopped in front of the Martinis' door. It was half open and inside one could see the tables set with pink cloths and stacks of paper cups. The doctor's voice just reached him: 'What are the haemoglobin levels? Are the platelets holding steady? Are there blast cells in the formula?' Pietro went down. The guests were seated, filling the courtyard in herringbone rows. Viola was next to her mother. He waved to Sara in the front row, surrounded by other children and Fernando. Riccardo was speaking with Paola between the stage and an improvised prop holding a speaker.

'Girls and boys, ladies and gentlemen, welcome!' The magician Nicolini wore a tailcoat with a yellow bow tie and a shiny top hat. He showed his empty hands to the audience, closed and reopened them three times, on the fourth time one hand held a silver knob. He shook it and out popped a walking stick. The guests applauded and so did the lawyer. Poppi was on the other side of the courtyard, Theo Morbidelli in his arms.

'So then, who wants to be my magical assistant?' Nicolini pointed his walking stick at the audience. All the children waved theirs arms to be chosen, as did the lawyer. The magician chose the birthday girl. 'A round of applause for Sara, a very special sorceress.' The child looked for her mother and started to laugh, looked for her father but didn't see him. Then she climbed timidly on stage.

Luca came down into the courtyard when his daughter was in the midst of the big finale. Held his mobile to his ear and watched Sara wave the magic wand that the magician had given her. She aimed it straight at the top hat, repeated abracadabra, and all the guests repeated abracadabra too, until from the top hat Nicolini pulled a dove, who perched on the little girl's shoulders. She screwed up her eyes in fright. The guests exploded with applause. Luca put away the phone and cheered on his daughter, then called Viola aside. He said something to her, they conferred, he walked away alone and returned up the stairs.

Pietro left the show when he realized the doctor was not coming back. Slipped into the entrance hall and glanced up the stairwell: no one. He could hear only the magician Nicolini announcing the number of flying handkerchiefs. The concierge climbed to the second floor. The Martinis' door was still open. In the living room Luca was pacing back and forth with a raincoat over his shoulder and rummaging in his leather bag.

Pietro knocked. 'Can I help?'

'It's Lorenzo . . .' The doctor was out of breath. 'He's worse. I received a call from the doctors attending him at home. I have to go right away.' He dropped the coat and bag and disappeared into the kitchen and returned with three trays of sweet pastries that he disposed haphazardly on one of the tables. 'Sara will never forgive me . . . At least I can make it so they'll find it all ready . . . All ready.' He was in a manic state. A tray slipped from his hand and he caught it in mid-air. Set it down and pulled away the wrapping paper.

'I'll take care of it.' Pietro tugged the second tray from his hands.

'Sara will never forgive me.'

'I'll take care of things here. Go.'

'OK, to hell with it.' The doctor picked up his bag and raincoat, turned on the threshold. 'You'll really take care of it?'

Pietro nodded and when Luca left stood alone at the centre of the living room. They had rearranged the furniture and removed the photo of the lavender field. He began with the longer trays, arranging them on the right-hand table and unwrapping them. Mixed petits fours, some with marzipan. He brought in other trays from the kitchen, one with cream meringues, another with Sicilian *cannoli*. There were also packaged cakes and other platters. He moved on to a strawberry tart, letting the ribbons and wrappers fall to the floor. The last items he found were cream puffs and iced rolls, which he squeezed onto the far edge of the central table. He touched his finger to the icing on a chocolate cream puff, broke off a piece and put it in his mouth, struggled to swallow. *Lorenzo is worse.* Knelt down to collect the tray wrappers, too late. Voices came from the landing. 'He left it open.' The voice was Viola's.

Pietro looked around, slipped into the hallway leading to

the bedrooms, and backed his way as far as Sara's room. Pressed himself against the wall as footsteps entered.

'What a mess Luca made of things,' Viola grumbled. 'You can never depend on him. What a mess.'

The concierge squatted down behind the child's bed. It was covered with dolls. More peeked out from beneath. The footsteps continued. He moved toward the foot of the bed, where the Pooh doll sat now.

'The little boy's condition must have taken a turn for the worse last night.' The other voice was Riccardo's. He gathered up the wrappers from the trays and gave them to Viola.

Pietro stretched out then retracted his legs. Squashed a cheek against the parquet floor, breathed in dust, sat up again.

'Sara will take it very badly.' Viola paced back and forth in the kitchen. 'Luca promised her he'd be here.'

Pooh's nose hid the woman's head. Pietro edged himself beyond the bed and saw her better. Viola took off her wrap and folded her arms, thrusting her chest forward. Riccardo's hands remained on his hips. 'Viola, listen to me.' He went up close to her. 'I can't take it any more.'

'Sara wanted all of us here today.'

'I'm not talking about today.'

Pietro slid forward.

Viola dropped her arms to her sides. 'Sara wanted all of us.'

'Sara says "father" to a man who is not her father.' Riccardo smothered a shout.

The concierge remained motionless.

'We're not going to do anything, Riccardo. Not now.'

'You want to keep deceiving him?' He cut the air with his hand. 'I won't go on like this.'

Pietro took hold of the foot of Winnie the Pooh.

'What's the point of telling him now . . .' Viola's voice was barely audible. 'What's the point, tell me.'

'A daughter . . .' the man said, 'ours.'

She leaned into Riccardo and he ran a hand over her hip, caressed her stomach and her chest. The hand undid a button of her blouse, slipped in, grasped. A breast emerged, white and majestic. They kissed.

The concierge turned: a tiny desk with crayons in a giant Smarties pot. He stared at the pot, the coloured bands at top and bottom. The voices in the living room died away and returned. Hers said not now, please, we have to go downstairs.

Riccardo left first. Viola fixed her shirt and covered herself again with the wrap, then she too left.

Pietro brought a hand to his eyes.

The mother of the witch did as her daughter did. That night she tossed a handful of gravel against the young priest's shutters. He got out of bed and saw her through the slits. He rushed to open the door to her. She removed a jumper she had wrapped around her head. Her face was red from the wind and her eyes were puffy. 'I couldn't wait, Father.'

He gestured for her to enter the church.

The woman went to the confessional.

'Forgive my sins.'

'Which sins?'

'A husband's.'

'Sins can't be passed on.'

'I've covered them up for years. Now they're mine.' The woman picked at the holes in the grille with her fingers. 'And my daughter's.'

He smelt the wine on her breath.

'My daughter leads others into temptation.'

The young priest touched his lips where they had kissed the witch. 'It's not your daughter's fault.'

'Whose is it, then?'

He backed away from the grille, hid himself in the shadow of the confessional. 'God's.'

Before the birthday party was over the guests were welcomed into the Martinis' living room, where the lawyer announced: 'This is Pietro and Fernando's gift for our guest of honour.'

The concierge had lowered the shutters and directed a lamp against the wall, set up two chairs in front of the light and returned to the kitchen. He came out with Fernando shortly after. The strange boy had his hands like Pietro had taught him. He sat down on one of the chairs and the concierge sat down on the other.

The guests applauded. Fernando sneezed and said, 'I'm scared, I'm scared.' He looked at Pietro, looked at his mother standing beside the door. Paola urged him on, along with Poppi, and blew him a kiss.

Fernando's parrot appeared on the wall, its mouth closed and missing its crest. The big boy's hands shook. The parrot threatened to become a flightless blotch. He straightened an index finger, it crumpled, the parrot fell. It rose again at the approach of Pietro's parrot, which was smaller and had its crest. The two met. The hands of the concierge brushed against Fernando's. The boy's parrot opened its beak. The crest emerged.

The guests applauded and Fernando turned towards his mother. His mother was laughing.

Pietro said, 'Fly away.'

Fernando moved his thumbs and spread the bird's wings. The concierge did the same, and they flew.

Pietro looked for her now. Viola was one silhouette among the others, picking at an apple torte, looking away to avoid his gaze.

# 29

Pietro returned from the birthday party with a kiss from Sara on his cheek and a tray of petits fours wrapped in crinkled paper. Through a gap he saw the top of a meringue. He slipped a finger into the package, found the whipped cream. Plunged in and brought the finger to his mouth as he looked at the ficus next to the refrigerator, entirely revived by the rain of the previous night. Took a pair of scissors from the table and knelt down. He pruned one green leaf after another, every leaf except the one with the shell. The snail had left a trail of slime across the veins.

The concierge rested the tray of petits fours on the Bianchi's handlebars, pocketed the photograph of the woman and newborn and went out into the courtyard with the bicycle. On the stage were three long balloons trampled flat. And Riccardo.

He blended in with the evening, until his cigarette glowed. The concierge turned to leave.

'Teach me how to make the shadows.' The man sat on the edge of the stage, dangling his legs. 'Teach me the parrot too.'

Pietro leaned on the top bar of the Bianchi. 'I can't do the parrot well any more.'

'Or whatever shadow you want . . .' He tossed the cigarette to the ground and hopped down from the stage. 'As long as it's different from my own.' The lamplight in the courtyard projected him on the ground in sharply angled silhouette.

'I can't do any of the shadows well any more.'

The radiographer came closer to him, stopping directly below the lamp. Pietro saw him clearly then. And recognized himself. Riccardo was an orphan. In the graceful gestures that smoothed the edges of an eternal awkwardness, in the cowed, anxious eyes from which he now brushed away curls. 'I trip over my own shadow.' He sniggered without smiling.

'So do I.' Pietro nodded as he had the first time they met. He knew that the awkwardness of this kind man was his own awkwardness. To be always alone. He laid a hand on his arm, just for a moment, and squeezed. Then he turned the Bianchi round and when he faced the street door he noticed a drawing stuck to the lodge window. Looking closer he made out a man sailing through the air on a red bicycle. Above the figure soared two lopsided birds with spikes on their heads. He pulled it down and read at the bottom, *Fernando and Sara*. Turned around and spied Fernando and Sara half hidden behind the stairs.

'For me?' the concierge asked.

The little girl ran to Pietro and tugged at the edge of his jacket, laughing, gap-toothed. Fernando stepped forward. 'It's a jewel,' he said, pointing to the drawing.

'Thank you very much.' The concierge ran a hand through the boy's hair. 'I'll hang it over my bed.'

Riccardo came over to them. 'They didn't know how to thank you, so they set to drawing as soon as the guests left.' He picked up the little girl.

Pietro stared at them, searching in the one, then in the

other. Sara had her mother's nose and eyes, her hands and way of laughing.

'I'm sleepy,' she murmured.

The concierge searched again. The child laid her head on Riccardo's shoulder and Pietro found the telltale sign. The pointed ear. A piece of cartilage sharpened her ear as it sharpened his. In the same curve, in the same way. Riccardo kissed her. 'Everyone to bed.'

Pietro caressed Sara's back, climbed his hand up to her shoulder, to her face. Brushed the ear there, said goodnight.

They went upstairs and he glanced at the Madonna in the alcove.

He asked now. That you might protect my son.

The entire ride, Pietro steered with one hand. The other steadied the tray of petits fours on the handlebars until he arrived at Anita's front gate, which had been left ajar. He buzzed. No one responded but he entered anyway, left the Bianchi in the rack and went up to the first floor. Rang at her door. The young woman came out of the flat next door. 'Anita will be here soon.'

'Thanks.' Pietro waited on a chair on the landing of the communal balcony. The young woman remained in the doorway of her flat, fiddling with her mobile phone, applying and reapplying lip gloss like the first time he'd met her. She wore a fringe nearly down to her eyes and two silver hoops in her ears. Pietro rested the tray on his knees, glimpsed the small cakes through the gap in the paper: they had all overturned. He uncovered the tray and began to right them. When he arrived at the strawberry petit four he looked up. The woman was smiling.

'Do you like the ones with fruit?' Pietro held out the tray to her and she chose the cake with the smallest strawberry. She nibbled at the edges and kept the fruit for last. 'Have you known Anita for a long time?'

'A lifetime.'

Her mobile rang and without answering the woman went to the intercom, pushed the button while she finished the petit four, looked down. Into the courtyard came a man in his fifties with his coat collar turned up. The man climbed to the second floor and hurried directly into the woman's flat. She followed him and before closing the door said, 'My name's Silvia.'

'Pietro.'

'Very pleased to meet you.' She locked the door and drew the curtain of her one window facing the communal balcony. The curtain was made of voile and through it he discerned her helping the man remove his coat and tie. Pietro stopped watching and stood up.

Anita smiled from the stairs. 'You were nice to Silvia.'

'Where were you?'

She showed him a bottle opener. 'I'd loaned it to my upstairs neighbour. I enjoyed your gallantry.' Anita lowered her voice: 'That's her third client today. Poor girl. Just think that I've seen her become like that in a year. Before she just studied and that was it.'

Pietro finished rewrapping the tray and gave it to her.

Anita kissed him on the cheek. 'What is it?'

The concierge waited until she opened her door, then as soon as they entered, embraced her. Dug his nose into her hair. Anita smelled of goodness.

'Something happened with your son, didn't it?'

The concierge pulled out the photograph of the woman with the newborn. He put it on the table.

Anita brought it up to the light. 'It's her. She's really beautiful.' She went over to Pietro and enunciated each word: 'Give the letter to your son. Tell him the truth.'

Anita took his hand. Led him into the bedroom, took off his jumper and trousers, unbuttoned his shirt. Went into the bathroom and when she returned he was as she had left him. Together they lay down on the bed, resting their heads on a single pillow. She pressed her breasts against him and he felt the tired flesh. They looked at each other. Pietro allowed himself to be kissed. Anita's lips tasted of goodness, too. Slowly he undressed her. Pushed her against the pillow. Anita said, 'Leave it to me,' but he held her still and himself above her. His hands roamed and fumbled. He sat up and they returned to his sides. She took his member in her hand, closed her fingers around it and gently shook the soft, yielding form. Pietro leaned forward to caress her neck. Began to squeeze it. 'Gently,' she said. Pietro squeezed and released, lowered himself onto her and took her broad face between his palms. Kissed her on the eyes.

Anita kissed him on the eyes as well. 'You deserve your son.'

Pietro pulled back. 'He deserves his daughter.'

# 30

Pietro left Anita's house at dawn. Before leaving, while she slept, he placed two marzipan petits fours on a small plate and prepared the stovetop percolator. As soon as it began to sputter he turned off the flame, went down into the courtyard and walked out with the Bianchi. He had always sought the dawn. In Rimini he would wake at night's end and walk down the Corso d'Augusto from the centre to the Tiberius Bridge, down into the fishermen's village with its pastel houses and low roofs. Emerge from the other end of the village and see the first slice of the harbour. Rimini at dawn is on tiptoe. He would tiptoe as well, waiting for the sun there, heels high, while the light lengthened the shadows of the only mother he had, his city.

From Anita's house the way was all downhill. The Bianchi flew through the large square with the clocks on skyscrapers and skirted the remains of the old city walls of Milan, arriving at the condominium as Alice pulled up the roller shutter of the cafe. She greeted him first, her eyes sleepy and the deliveries from the bakery piled up at the entrance. Pietro carried them in for her.

Alice turned on the lights above the counter. 'I saw you with the doctor the other evening.' She lifted an apron over her neck and fiddled with the cash register.

He looked at her, a woman full of grace who merely grazed the world as she moved. She unwrapped the pastries and arranged them in the display case as if without touching them. 'There's some Mastroianni in the doctor as well . . . The three of you resemble each other.' She blew the powdered sugar from her hands. 'How about a croissant and some hot chocolate? What do you say, Marcello? It's on the house. These are my last days on the job.'

Pietro smiled at her and backed away. He left the cafe and directly he arrived in the street ran a hand over his face, over his nose and over his mouth. Brought the Bianchi into the condominium and started up the stairs. Touched his ears and his forehead, his hair. Reached the first floor and the second, climbed further and his fingers continued to seek out the resemblance with his son. He climbed the stairs to the top, found the iron door slightly ajar, opened it wide and arrived on the terrace. Slipped between the sheets and waited for the sun as he had waited for it for years. When it rose he clicked his heels and returned onto his toes, clicked them again, the start of a routine that had no need of any music. He finished abruptly and the moment he came to a stop, someone applauded. Pietro turned around, saw no one. Ducked under a sheet. The lawyer sat on the parapet wall. 'Celeste told me about the rhythm in those shoes.'

The young priest saw the witch again at mass. She sat in the third row with her mother, head bowed and hands interlaced on her belly. He looked at her from the altar, then raised up the blood and body of Christ, consumed them. Began to place the wafers in the mouths of the faithful. The organ played hallelujah, hallelujah. The witch was the last in line. He continued to place the wafers in mouths, in the mouths of the faithful, in the mother's mouth, then he found the witch standing before him. Picked up the wafer and offered it to her. In exchange he received a strip of paper. The young priest looked at it when he returned behind the altar. Hallelujah, hallelujah. He read: *Tonight at 11, the fountain with the four horses.*

The lawyer rose from the parapet. He was in his dressing gown and smoking. 'Don't be so surprised, my friend.' His face was severe, unadorned, old. 'I have the spirit of a confessor. Celeste, on the other hand, was a sharer of confidences.'

Pietro remained motionless, then swiftly hid himself behind a flannel sheet. The scent of fabric softener was everywhere. His voice wouldn't come, came and was barely audible. 'What confidences?'

'I'm sorry, I forget.' Poppi came forward in his silk slippers. 'The passion for dance – this I remember.'

'I don't know how to dance.' Pietro found himself face to face with the lawyer.

'Neither do I.' The slippers rose up on their heels. 'Except when I'm scared. Or I miss my Daniele.' He passed through the sheets until he reached a kind of chimney at the centre of the terrace. It supported two satellite dishes. He pointed to the concrete base. 'We would come here to smoke. He didn't want us to in the house.' There was something written in chalk on the concrete: *Giovanni Poppi & Daniele Izzo.* 'Memory makes the feet move, isn't that right?'

The concierge looked at him.

'Tell me why God carried away the love of my life, Pietro.' His lips trembled. He tossed the cigarette. 'Tell me what's left behind. Ask your god, c'mon.'

'It's not my god.'

'What's left, Pietro?'

The concierge went to the parapet. Down in the street, he could see, Alice had turned on the neon signs. A few of the tables were already filled. 'Memory is what's left.'

'The great lie, that's what memory is.' Poppi screened his eyes against the light. 'Let the Lord try to get by on memory, then he'll know what punishment is.' And without warning he approached Pietro, took and raised his hands, began to lead him in a weary waltz. Pulled him over to the sheets. 'Do you know what the Jews say, my friend? *Mazel tov*. Good luck.' They continued the unsteady dance. '*Mazel tov* to us survivors.' They stopped and the scent of Poppi enveloped the concierge. Poppi's mouth brushed Pietro's ear, his hands still in Pietro's hands: 'Go and find Celeste, I'll tell you where she is. Less than a metre of earth won't keep you apart.'

# 31

Lorenzo died that morning. The lodge phone rang around ten. Pietro did not hear it. He was working in the courtyard with the radio on, cleaning up the mess from the birthday party. When they called the second time the concierge had returned to his flat to change. He put a towel around his shoulders and went into the lodge to answer. 'Hello,' he said. The towel slipped to the floor and he remained bare-chested with the receiver at his ear.

Paola passed by in that moment, spotted him and opened one of the newspapers she had just bought, pretended to read it as she approached the lodge.

The concierge was facing away from her. 'What's the address?' he asked into the phone, writing the reply on a supermarket flyer. 'I'll come right away.' He hung up.

Paola entered the lodge. 'Oh, pardon me, oh . . . I wanted to check if any post had come for me, I didn't see you.'

'The phone rang while I was changing.' Pietro picked up the towel and opened her letterbox, gave her three letters.

She placed them in her purse. There was an acrid smell. She breathed it in, removed her hat, breathed again. 'You were an angel to show my Fernando how to make the shadows.'

'I have to go, Paola.'

'I haven't seen him like that since his father was alive.' She laid a hand on his naked shoulder.

'I have to go.' He left her there, went back into his flat and finished changing in a hurry. The Bianchi wouldn't do. When he came out again the lodge was empty and the acrid odour mixed with that of paint.

He went into the street and waited at the light. Two engaged taxis passed. He hailed the third one. Got in and read out the address he had written down.

The house where Lorenzo lived appeared lifeless. Pietro got out of the taxi and approached the art-nouveau villa. The front gate clicked open before he could buzz. The doctor emerged immediately and walked up to him. 'It's since yesterday that he's been getting worse.' He grasped his shoulder. 'Since yesterday.'

Pietro looked at Luca. He was a wreck. A drooping reed. The concierge followed him up the path to the villa. Its shutters were closed and the lawn perfectly groomed.

They went inside. A housemaid was waiting for them beside a vase of fresh calla lilies. She took Pietro's coat and led them down a broad, dimly lit hallway, interrupted three-quarters along by a couch with paw-shaped brass feet and an end table covered with magazines. The freshly painted walls smelled old. Two doctors emerged from a room, called Luca aside. 'Wait for me here, Pietro.'

The concierge waited in front of an electric fireplace. The false flame glowed behind glass. Above the mantelpiece hung an oil painting of Lorenzo posing with his mother and a Dalmatian as tall as he was.

Luca returned. 'Let's go.' And he proceeded to the end of the hall.

She was there. Leaning against the door frame, more beautiful than the portrait with the Dalmatian. She had her hair tied back and a shawl that brushed the floor, a teddy bear in her hands. She herself was a doll with vacant eyes and a rigid neck, staring at the floor. Stared now at Pietro and said nothing, turning just slightly.

Luca touched her shoulder. 'Giulia, this is Pietro.'

The doll opened her mouth slightly. She wore no lipstick. 'He wasn't baptized.' Torment faintly spoiled her face. Grace remained in her frightened gestures. She stroked the teddy bear. 'My son wasn't baptized.'

Luca opened the door to the room. In the middle was a four-poster bed draped with light blue chiffon. On the walls a poster with lions, another with monkeys. In the corner a clown made of fabric. On the far side a table with folded clothes and a picture book: *The Animals of the Savannah*. From the windows, their shades half drawn, could be seen a field of nothing but weeds. The light was failing.

Lorenzo was a tiny ball of a thing, curled up on his side under a dark blue blanket. When he left his head was bent nearly to his chest, leaving the blanket halfway up a face whose paleness had become pink. Luca pushed aside the chiffon and sat down on the bed. Pietro remained standing and watched his son caressing the son of another. The doctor pinched the child's leg through the covers and gently shook him, *My dear little boy,* lowered the sheet to free his face. His hand grazed Lorenzo from forehead to chin, then he turned him on his back with his arms along his sides. He made space for Pietro.

The priest came forward. He perched on the mattress and stroked Lorenzo's cheek as he had at the lake, and as on that day he closed a hand over one of the child's hands. The cut on the thumb was almost healed. Pietro rubbed it and turned toward the mother.

She continued to stand in the doorway, hands around the teddy bear, hands raw in the fingers, raw at the knuckles from scratching. Her face of porcelain. The woman threatened to fade from visibility, transparent in the same way as her son. 'I'm here,' she murmured and at the same time backed further away.

The priest pressed the pillow down and settled Lorenzo's head at its centre. Only then did he see it: the elephant that he had given him peeked out between the mattress and the headboard, its feet in the air and its trunk buried in the folds of the sheet. He placed it beside him. 'It's here,' he said, and made it so that one foot touched the child, because that was the sense of the elephant and of all fathers, their devotion to all sons. He held Lorenzo from above, in the hollow of his arms, squeezed and was afraid of hurting him.

The other doctors called Luca and he went to them. The mother retreated further, becoming a mere porcelain shadow in the doorway. She stared at the bedroom window and squeezed the teddy bear. Met the priest's gaze, looked away when the child's mouth abruptly fell open. The priest clamped it shut and said, 'Take him with you, O Lord, because you are the Father he wants and he is the son you want.' He made the sign of the cross and placed a hand over the boy's eyes.

*

Lorenzo's mother held on to the door jamb. Then she slowly came forward, her dress encumbering her walk. Dropped her shawl and pushed aside the chiffon of the canopy, stretched out a hand and touched the little one's neck. It was still warm. She touched an arm and his ribs beneath his pyjamas, so hard. Then she recognized her son.

'My child.'

Her voice was weary, her grace lost. She slipped off her shoes and sat down. Gently shook the child and lay down beside him. She put the teddy bear in his arms and rested her cheek against his smooth head. 'God takes from the ungrateful.'

Pietro backed away.

The mother collapsed onto her son.

# 32

A bluish strip in the west was all that remained of the day. The concierge left the villa ahead of Luca and when he was in the street he searched his coat. He drew out the elephant. He had taken it even as the mother gazed at her son and called him her child. Pietro held it in both hands, noticed that the trunk and feet had been gnawed on, felt the traces of Lorenzo's teeth. When he got in the car he saw that Luca was already inside, leaning his head against the window. The doctor started the car and slowly drove down the street, went round the block, turned again and returned them to their starting place. The light over the villa's entrance had gone on, so too several lights behind its windows. Luca stared at them. 'All you need to survive is one decent memory. His mother probably has one.'

Pietro protected the elephant's trunk in his fingers, closed them over it. They set off again. They took the street that ran along the park and led to the airport. The rows of houses rhythmically notched the sky. Luca bumped his head back against the headrest, a puppet without strings, bent forward and straightened up again, collapsed. 'Every time one of my children died I would go to my mother.' He could not cry, rubbed his eyes and sounded the horn at the cars stuck under the flyover. Changed lanes, accelerated. 'I'd go to her.' Stretched his neck and half-closed his eyes. 'Now I go to whom I have left.'

Pietro recognized the street. 'Viola.'

Now Luca nodded and, halfway down the street, slowed. Slowed further as he ran his wooden hands down the steering wheel from top to bottom. Dropped them in his lap and took his foot off the accelerator. A gurgling rose from his mouth. He lowered the window and steered over to the shoulder of the road. He breathed with difficulty, gasped and coughed. The crying came upon him, a sobbing without tears. He tried to say something, mumbled. Mumbled again: 'I've always known about them. About her and Riccardo. I didn't want to lose them.'

The car came to a complete stop.

Pietro was looking through the windscreen. The evening had consumed the bluish streak. He looked at Luca, who had dropped his chin to his chest. They resembled each other in the dimple in the right cheek, the forehead crease.

Luca's face was calm. The murmur of the car's engine drowned out his deep breaths. He wiped his eyes and extended an arm toward the concierge.

Pietro felt the cold wood, warmed it between his hands.

The young priest arrived at the fountain on his bike. The witch was waiting for him, seated Indian-style. The four horses, sculpted with their rears joined in the centre, snorted water from their nostrils. He braked to a stop and dismounted before her. 'What do you have to say to me?'

The music of a seaside dance hall reached them. The witch stood and ran through a few steps. 'There's not much to say in a goodbye.'

'This is goodbye?'

'You belong to the Lord. And I've already committed the greatest sin.' She touched her stomach. 'I'm made of remorse.'

'And I of regrets.' He pulled away and made to climb back on the bike.

She grabbed a handlebar. The water in the horses' nostrils stopped.

'Stop here, please,' said Luca.

Pietro parked in front of a terraced house with a yellow facade. He had taken the doctor's place behind the wheel after he had said he couldn't manage. He glanced now through the window at the house. 'Who lives there?'

Luca fixed his hair and shirt. Before getting out he looked down at his trembling hands. Got out and rang the doorbell. The door opened and he disappeared inside. Re-emerged shortly after with Sara clinging to his neck, giving him a series of kisses on his head and holding him tight.

'Did you have fun at Grandma and Grandpa's, honey?' Luca sat her in the back and returned to his place in the front. The child paid no attention to the concierge and shuffled toward her father's seat. Squinted at him, shook her index finger like a magic wand, abracadabra. Touched first one of his eyes, then another.

'Did you see Pietro's here?'

But she continued to peer at the distressed face of her father, hugged him as best she could. When the car set off again she pushed further forward and took better hold of him. And her father said to her,

*Don't be afraid*
*It's just the dark*
*A bit of colour*
*A great inky gloom*
*Don't be afraid*
*It's just the sun*
*Who's yawning because*
*He wants to sleep*

Sara sang softly along with him. Then again as she settled back on the seat. And again moments before falling asleep. Luca repeated it on his own, *Don't be afraid, it's just the dark, a bit of colour, a great inky gloom,* until they parked in front of the condominium. Then picked up his daughter, entered the building and climbed the stairs.

The concierge accompanied them to the second floor. 'I'll be up if you need me.'

Luca cleared his throat. 'There's a man . . .' He spoke quietly. 'A man . . . I have to visit him in two days. He lives in your city. I need someone who knows the area.'

Pietro remained silent.

'Come with me to Rimini.'

Sara lifted her head from her father's shoulder.

'It's for work, honey. You get bored when Daddy works.' Luca scratched the back of her neck. 'Come with me, Pietro. Your sea will be there as well.'

The concierge looked at them together. A father and his daughter. The crying had left its mark on Luca's face, still slightly swollen. Sleepiness weighed down the eyes of both of them. Sara pressed her cheek, stuck her ear to his. Hers alone had the pointed tip.

Luca waited for an answer. When it didn't come he entered his flat, begging Pietro's pardon, and closed the door.

'Goodnight.' The concierge returned to the lodge. Sat down in front of the window and opened the curtains. Pulled out the elephant, placed it at the centre of the table.

The witch leapt to the rim of the fountain, did a pirouette. 'Witches dance at goodbyes. Priests cry.'

The young priest brought a finger to his dry eyes. 'I'm not crying.'

'But you're not a priest.'

He stood back on his heels, tapped up and down.

The witch laughed. 'That's how you defy Heaven?'

Pietro went to her and gently lifted her up and settled her on the Bianchi. He got on and began to pedal. 'This is how.'

During the night the doctor came down into the condominium's entrance hall. Pietro was asleep in the lodge's wicker chair. He woke when Luca tossed the duffel bag to the floor. Stood and saw his son carrying a second duffel, his leather medical bag and a plastic bag containing a limp quilt and orange sheets. The doctor's face was crêpe paper, his eyes two glass marbles. He held them open wide, closed them and turned toward the stairs. 'Viola, go back inside.'

Light footsteps climbed as the sound of a car came from the other side of the street door. Luca picked up the two duffel bags and went out to the street. 'I have other things, please wait.'

Pietro took the other things. Carried out the plastic bag and the leather bag. Loaded them into the boot of the taxi that was parked outside, hazard lights flashing. 'Where will you go, Doctor?'

'Nearby.'

Luca leaned toward the concierge and wrapped an arm around him. Climbed into the taxi. Pietro waited on the pavement for it to leave before going back inside.

Viola was a shadow on the stairs. 'He's left us . . . Did he tell you where he's going?'

He shook his head.

She started up. 'What will I tell my child . . .'

# 33

*Ffffff*, Pietro felt blowing in his ear. *Ffffff*, he opened his eyes wide and raised his head from the lodge table.

'They had a fight.' Fernando, leaning through the lodge window, blew one last time and stroked the concierge's forehead.

Pietro checked his watch and smoothed down his hair. Behind Fernando he could see Paola. 'I nodded off,' he told her.

'I didn't get any sleep myself last night. You saw him leave, didn't you?' She clinked the bracelets at her wrist. 'Good heavens.'

'Good heavens,' Fernando echoed.

'When I heard them crying my heart just stopped.' Paola tossed her hair back and squeezed the handbag she held beneath one arm. Turned to watch Poppi coming down the stairs. The lawyer removed his hat. His face was dark. He avoided Paola's eyes and sought out those of the concierge. His sneer was gone. He tried to speak, gave up.

'Pietro saw Luca leave. It's terrible.' Paola hugged her son and walked toward the exit. She was reaching for the button when the street door opened on its own. A headful of curls and a hand holding a paper bag entered. It was Riccardo.

Pietro looked through the closed pane of the lodge window. The radiographer was like a distorted reflection, growing larger. 'One chocolate croissant for the cyclist.' Riccardo dropped the bag in and started up the stairs.

'I'll catch up with you at the cafe, Paola. Go on ahead.' The lawyer lit a cigarette.

She looked him up and down, unable to decide. When she did leave with Fernando, Pietro brought Poppi an ashtray. 'I need to ask for a day off. The day after tomorrow' – he paused – 'I'm going with the doctor to Rimini.'

Poppi loosened his tie, arched an eyebrow.

'He has to meet a patient and needs someone who knows the area,' the concierge said.

The lawyer sucked down more smoke and drew him close. 'You and I are going up to my place. Right now.'

'For what?'

'I have a plant that's not doing well.'

'Can't this wait till the afternoon?'

'Now.'

They went up. The lawyer opened the door and invited him in, walked across the living room and hauled a cycad in a pot to the entryway. The leaves came to sharp points, which were in fact dry.

'I'll take care of it.'

Poppi put out his cigarette in the earth around the plant. Held the concierge there without saying anything, without doing anything, and when Pietro tried to speak he pointed to the wall he shared with the Martinis. They heard the muffled voice of Riccardo.

Then Viola spoke. She said that he left last night, he really did it. *He left with hardly a word. Luca knew everything.*

*Luca has always known everything.*

Pietro bent over the cycad and tried to lift it but the lawyer prevented him with a foot on the rim of the pot.

*Now we have to tell him about Sara, Viola.*

*Not now. I want to protect him.*

Poppi caressed a tribal mask on the wall, bowed his head. His cranium was a gleaming knob.

*Protect him like you've done so far?*

*Luca needs Sara right now. Today he's going to pick her up from nursery school and tonight she'll sleep at his place.*

*When are we going to tell him, Viola?*

The lawyer slipped two fingers through the eye sockets of the mask and squeezed.

When Pietro came down from the lawyer's flat he went straight to the lodge and checked the condominium register. Turned to the page with the resident notes from the previous concierge. There were five for the Martinis, the penultimate of which was *Sara, Crivelli Nursery, ask for Mrs Rita*. There was the address, telephone number, and the name of the person in charge. He checked the time and looked up the street in the street guide, left with the Bianchi. Came to a quick halt on the pavement.

The old man from the petrol station stood in front of the intercom button grid. 'I didn't risk buzzing.' He was wearing nice clothes, a woollen jacket and newly polished shoes. 'I wanted to say hi.' The man held out his hand.

The concierge shook it. 'My son is not home.'

'I wanted to say hi to you.' He coughed, dabbed his lips

with a handkerchief and waited for Pietro knew not what. Then mumbled, 'Please just tell the doctor that I don't have much time left. Please tell him that.' Moved away little by little, disappeared around the corner.

The concierge mounted the Bianchi and pushed off into the street, pedalling with difficulty during the entire trip. When he arrived he noticed how weak he was. Leaned the Bianchi against a tree and rubbed his face. Sara's nursery school was in a house with a garden at the front. The gate was covered with plastic panels and on each panel was an image of Jiminy Cricket. A group of people waited out front. Luca stood apart from the group, pacing back and forth on the pavement, kicking a stone and returning it to its original location. Struck it again, greeted a man smoking a cigar. They spoke together quietly until joined by a young woman with a dog on a leash.

The gate opened and Luca entered alongside the young woman and the man. Returned with Sara, hand in hand. The girl could barely keep up with her father, so he slipped off her schoolbag and carried it over his shoulder. They walked beneath the horse-chestnut trees, through the fallen leaves on the pavement, leaving shuffled footprints. Arrived in the university district and turned down a cobbled alley, stopping in front of a small block of flats with tiled balconies.

Sara saw Pietro for the first time. She made her father put her down, skipped over to the concierge.

The doctor stood with a set of keys hanging from his little finger. 'Pietro.'

'I had passed by the nursery and you . . .'

'What's happened?'

'I'm coming to Rimini.'

The doctor cracked a smile, readjusted the pack on his back. 'Poppi asked me if he could come as well. He heard about it from you.'

Pietro screwed up his face and stayed silent. 'Sorry, it slipped out when I asked him for the day off.'

Luca looked preoccupied, without moving, then asked Pietro to follow him inside.

The entrance hall had frescoes on the walls, beyond that a negligible courtyard, then the garden of an independent residence. Luca opened wide the two leaves of a small door next to the main entrance, led them up a few steps and down a corridor with three doors. Tried to insert the key into the lock of the first. His hand shook and could not find the target.

Pietro helped him.

'Once upon a time my father let it to students.' He pressed down on the handle. The child ran inside and around the piles of luggage. It was a bare studio, white, with a high table and four stools near the cooking corner, a blue couch against the wall. There was a glassed-in loft with a double bed. The windows looked out onto the street. A tram passed and the wooden floor began to vibrate. Sara scrambled up the narrow steps leading to the loft and continued to explore.

'I was wondering, Pietro . . .' Luca bent over the baggage, began to search at random. Slipped his hand into bag after bag without pulling out anything, without seeing anything. His eyes were empty. He covered them with a hand and went to the window. The heads of passers-by appeared in the lower part of the glass. 'I was wondering if you were afraid when you left God.'

Sara climbed halfway down the steps and called her father over, made him sit on the step in front of her, began to comb his hair with her hands.

The concierge approached. 'I've never stopped being afraid.'

Luca closed his eyes while Sara pulled tufts of hair down flat on his forehead. 'For the trip to the coast, how about we meet here the day after tomorrow at eight?'

Pietro nodded.

'And me?' asked the daughter.

# 34

The young priest stood up on the pedals. The witch perched sideways in front of him on the bicycle's top bar and her scarf fluttered out behind her. It flew off into his face: witches smell like fresh flowers. The bicycle creaked, *chk-chk*. He headed toward the music coming from the dance hall. She held tight to the handlebars. 'What make is this bike?'

'It's a Bianchi.' He accelerated again.

'And does it have brakes?'

He didn't touch them and the Bianchi flew past beach after beach, into a fog bank, *chk-chk*. They hurtled by and the witch counted the numbers of the beaches, number five, number four. He rang his bell loudly at a man cutting across his path and the man saw only fog pass. The young priest took a hand off the handlebars, rested it on her stomach, beach number one, then the open sand. He kept it there until they arrived at the inlet next to the jetty, where four strings of lights marked out a tiny plot of sand crowded with people spinning.

He slowed down.

The Bianchi had good brakes, which Pietro slammed on now. On the other side of the boulevard three cars queued at the petrol station. The first was being filled by the old man. Pietro stood on the pedals and continued past, turning into a cross-street and turning again, onto the street parallel to the boulevard. He left the bike against one of the sycamores and walked the path along the railway to the improvised gardens. The fence alongside the plot belonging to the old man from the petrol station was broken down at one point. Pietro hopped over it and his feet sank into the earth. The two pomegranate trees were leafless and without fruit. He went closer. To either side were rows of cabbage and lettuce. The whistle of a freight train approached. The smaller pomegranate tree was the same height as the concierge. Pietro went up to it and grasped the two branches that split from the trunk. He squeezed and felt that the wood was dust, crumbling in his hands. Squeezed again and raised his head toward the ugly building. There was a light in Andrea's window.

The young priest braked to a stop thirty paces from the dance floor. Music blasted from a plywood shack. The witch jumped down, saying, 'They'll see us,' and pressed herself against him. Crouched down and stroked his calves, took off first one of his shoes, then the other. Stood up and leaned the Bianchi against a tree, remaining to stare at the leaves.

'What are you looking at?' asked the young priest.

The witch brought her eyes closer to the tree. 'Mama says that it's the fruit of the Promised Land.' She broke off an unripe pomegranate and slammed it against the handlebars, splitting the fruit open. 'It has six hundred and thirteen seeds, as many as the rules of the Lord. Some represent sacrifice, some represent grace. Shall we try?' She gave half of the pomegranate to the young priest and leaned against the tree. 'If it's sweet, it's a grace. If it's sour, it's a sacrifice.' She sucked on a seed and said, 'Good.' Another and said, 'Good.' Yet another and said, 'Good. Three graces.'

The young priest put one in his mouth and it burned on his tongue. He spat it out.

The house of the pomegranate trees was mute. Pietro pressed the button next to the names *Mario and Andrea Testi.*

'Who is it?' The voice of Snow White crackled through the intercom.

'It's Pietro. Dr Martini's father.'

'Mr Mario isn't here.'

'I wanted to see Andrea.'

The intercom continued to crackle.

'I wanted to see him.'

The door clicked open and Pietro went up. Snow White was waiting for him in front of the flat. 'Andrea is happy to see the doctor's father.' The young woman had her hair loose and wore a close-fitting tracksuit. She invited him in.

The entry smelled of cleaning products. Pietro took off his jacket and folded it over his arm, asked if he could go in.

'Andrea's awake. He's watching TV that makes him laugh.' She led him to the room at the end of the hallway, asked him to wait outside. Entered alone and turned down the volume on the television.

Pietro could make out half a bed, an argyle blanket hiding the shrivelled legs.

Snow White came out and motioned the concierge forward, stopping him on the threshold. 'He answers "yes" if his eyes go white once, "no" if twice. He never closes his eyes ever or almost.'

Pietro approached the bed. Andrea had something behind his neck that kept him facing the screen. A cartoon was playing.

'*Ciao*, Andrea.'

His hair was combed, his face a mound of sagging flesh. His pupils went up once, looking at the Bristol set against the whiteboard on the wall, on it a sketch of two rows of seagulls and strip of sea.

Pietro pointed to the Bristol. 'The drawing is very nice.'

The eyes went white twice.

'But it is.'

There was an armchair beside the bed. Pietro removed a fashion magazine and sat down. 'I come from the sea and I know seagulls well.'

Snow White caressed Andrea's head. 'I'm going into the kitchen. I'll come back in a bit to see if everything is going OK.'

They heard her walk down the hallway. Pietro half-closed the door. Took hold of the hissing tube that terminated in the young man's throat. It was plastic and vibrated with each breath.

'I know you like football.'

The eyes went white and agonizingly wide.

Pietro looked out the window. A veil of fog had descended. He crossed the room. The whiteboard had a reading lamp below it. 'I also know that you like motorcycles.' Pietro stroked one of Andrea's arms, a forgotten stick, from elbow to hand. 'Your father told me everything. He very much likes to talk.'

The pupils rose.

Pietro smiled. Rubbed the arm again but the chill wouldn't leave the skin, covered it with the sheet. Turned on the lamp and directed it toward the wardrobe and placed his hands in front. The shadows of the parrot and the dog came out less lopsided than usual and no longer shivered. He turned around. Andrea was staring at them.

'A woman I know taught me how to make them.' He lowered the left sidewall and sat down on the mattress, took the tube back in hand, flattened it and one of the machines began to whistle. The young man's breath began to whistle as well. Pietro released the tube and there were no further sounds.

Snow White appeared in the doorway, stepped into the room. 'You can't be on the mattress, Mr Pietro.'

The concierge replaced the sidewall. Snow White nodded and returned whence she had come.

'Sofia is pretty.' He moved to the end of the bed, to the spot where Andrea's eyes were looking.

Pietro looked at him as well. 'Do you want to die, my son?'

The eyes were opened wide, and raised. Once.

# 35

That night in the studio flat Sara asked, 'Why doesn't Mama come here?'

Luca murmured, 'Take deep breaths, honey. That way you'll fall asleep sooner. *Don't be afraid, it's just the dark, a bit of colour, a great inky gloom. Don't be afraid, it's just the sun, who's yawning because he wants to sleep*.' They sang together and then she whispered, 'Will you take me to the sea?'

'You've got to go to nursery school. We'll go to the sea this summer, right now it's cold.' He rocked her in his arms and she said, 'I want to come with you to the cold sea.'

The deep breaths began but no one fell asleep in the studio flat, nor in the house of the pomegranate trees. The old man from the petrol station lowered one of the bed's sidewalls and lay down next to his son. *You and I, we're like Rossi and Altobelli against Germany, world champions, like Rossi and Altobelli, we take everyone by surprise*. The father closed his eyes and coughed. The son raised his pupils once. His voice echoed in the concierge's lodge. From the recorder came the crackling voice: 'My name is Andrea Testi. I am thirty-four years old and I know how to dribble. You have to have strong ankles to dribble well, and I have strong ankles.' Pietro listened to it again and again as he stared at the letter on rice paper held down by the elephant and by the pomegranate. Dozed off, then the voice of Andrea was silent and Pietro slept until the following morning.

He was woken by Riccardo's knock on the door.

The concierge opened. Riccardo stood there with a stuffed animal in one hand and a black raincoat fastened up to his neck. Gave a slight smile. 'Pardon me, you were sleeping.'

Pietro nodded.

'It's Lorenzo's funeral. If you want, I'll give you a ride. The church is a little out of the way.'

The concierge motioned for him to sit down on a wicker chair and went into the bathroom. Rinsed his face. It was lean and had lost its greyness. What remained of Mastroianni were the bags under his eyes and the forehead crease. He dressed in a hurry, placed the elephant in his jacket in a way that the trunk emerged over the edge of the pocket. Before going out he stuck Fernando and Sara's drawing above his bed. The two parrots were crippled and the Bianchi a tricycle with punctured tyres. He pressed it hard against the wall then drew out the leather bracelet from the night table and returned to the lodge. Riccardo was reading a completed crossword puzzle. Now he rose from the wicker chair and went out. Pietro hung the 'Back soon' sign on the window glass and joined him outside.

They climbed into the SUV parked outside the street door. A miniature tennis racket hung from the rear-view mirror. In the receptacle between the seats were some wadded-up receipts, covered in ash. Riccardo placed the animal in his lap and started the car. When they set off the toy fell over and he straightened it up. 'I didn't think Luca had said anything to you.' His face was hard. 'When he loses a child he closes out the world.'

'The same thing can happen when someone loses a wife.'

The SUV slowed. Riccardo stared straight ahead. Clutched the animal's trunk, opening and closing his fingers, then took the wheel with both hands, accelerated and cleared his throat. Turned his head toward the passenger side. 'We fell in love, Pietro.'

The concierge looked out the side window. The city was stuck in ice. 'I understand.'

'You understand?'

He nodded. 'People leave each other because at some point someone decides to try someone else.' His fingers grazed the elephant. 'It's minimal love.'

Riccardo looked at the road and then again at the concierge. 'And what would maximum love be?'

'To stand by the love of a single person.'

'Sometimes you can't.'

'Because sometimes you don't want to.'

'You speak as a priest.'

'I speak as an old man.'

He tapped his fingers on the steering wheel. 'So with God it was minimal?'

'It wasn't love.'

'So why did you become a priest?'

'Because I'd never known anything else.'

The elephant smashed its trunk against the horn. Riccardo wedged it between his legs and the SUV went through a yellow light. 'I didn't know anything else, either, after I lost my parents.' He drove along a section of one of the inner ring roads, unable to find a parking spot, made turn after fruitless turn, finally pulled into a spot for residents. Through the window they could see the beginning of the pedestrian zone, a group of people proceeding slowly into a red-brick church. Riccardo leaned over to Pietro's side and opened the glove box. Out popped a city street map, a Michelin restaurant guide and a GPS device. He searched haphazardly, saying, 'Where did I put it.' There was also a prescription pad and a plastic case with the car's papers. He opened the latter and a Polaroid fell and landed face down just under the seat. Pietro retrieved it and Riccardo took it out of his hands. 'I want to have a family again, Pietro.' He put the photograph away and continued to rummage, more calmly now. Extracted from the back of the glove box a doctor's badge and placed it next to the parking disc.

'All Luca needs is his daughter.' He handed him the bracelet.

Riccardo gave him a bewildered look, took the bracelet and held it in the palm of his hand. 'That's not how things are.' He attached it to his wrist.

'All Luca needs is his daughter.' The concierge began to get out. Riccardo took hold of his sleeve. 'Would God absolve me?'

'God doesn't understand such things.'

'Would you absolve me?'

'I'm only a man.'

Pietro walked ahead of him toward the church. People were entering in dribs and drabs. Two beggars shook their cups and asked for charity in the corner reserved for flowers. Riccardo left the toy between two wreaths of white roses. The concierge began to follow a group of women crowding the entrance, then stopped. Luca appeared among them, zipped up tight in a heavy jacket and wearing running shoes.

Riccardo, too, noticed him. 'Luca,' he called, 'Luca.'

The doctor moved away, darting into the church courtyard, five bare trees and a carpet of earth. Riccardo called him again, made to follow. This time it was the concierge who held him back.

'I have to talk to him, Pietro.'

The concierge refused to let him go. They walked together into the church, then Riccardo squirmed free to join Lorenzo's mother beside the casket. She had her hand inside the white box and was saying something to a lanky priest wearing a gown that was too short.

Pietro placed himself just inside the right aisle, beside a minor Christ who looked at him sidelong. He had not entered a church since he left his own. He rubbed his hands together. The chill in his bones had returned. Below the ankles of the minor Christ trembled the flames of the votive candles. The prayers melted over the rusty iron.

Everyone sat down except for Lorenzo's mother. She remained in place, one hand fussing with a pearl earring, the other stroking the casket.

'Let us pray,' announced the priest.

Pietro lowered his eyes to the marble floor, counted granules in the stone while the priest raised his hands to the heavens, *Let us pray*. Lorenzo's mother prayed, as did Riccardo in the second row and the rest of the people with heads bowed in the pews. The doctor prayed, seated in the church courtyard, running shoes nestled in the earth. Luca pressed his hands to his eyes and kept them there, and Lorenzo's mother did the same. They both said: 'Why me.'

# 36

The departure for Rimini was set for eight. Pietro arrived at the studio flat ten minutes early. The flat's shutters were closed. He waited outside the street door, a backpack in hand, wearing a coat that would keep out the cold. The day before, after Lorenzo's funeral, he had passed by Anita's shop to let her know: 'I'm returning to the sea for a few hours. With my son.' She smiled and asked, 'When you're there, will you do me a small favour?' He accepted and Anita gave him an empty jam jar.

Pietro checked the backpack to make sure he had brought the jar. When he looked up he noticed them. The doctor and the little girl were sitting at the window in the cafe across the street. Sara was wiping her father's mouth. He was doing the same to hers. Each held half a doughnut in hands covered in powdered sugar. The concierge crossed the street and knocked on the glass. A second later, a silver MPV with *Deluxe Vans* on its side parked in front of the flat. He looked at his watch: eight o'clock on the dot.

The lawyer stepped down from behind the wheel, waving a fur hat topped with a peacock feather. He turned around, walked toward Pietro and bowed before him. Paola lowered the van window to greet him. 'Don't get out, Fernando,' she said, shaking her newly permed head. But Fernando was already out, wearing his beret and with a camera around his neck. He captured the scene of the lawyer bowing to the concierge, behind them the arriving Luca and his daughter.

Poppi, a corner of his mouth rising, approached the doctor. 'We're coming to the sea too.' He shook the doctor's hand. The weighty fur hat swayed, straining his giraffe's neck.

Luca set down Sara's schoolbag and his medical bag. Dangled car keys from an index finger. 'It's for work, Mr Poppi.'

'We're a family, Doctor.'

'It's for work, I already told you on the phone.'

'You also told me what time you were leaving. And this I call a subconscious request for support. Don't worry, while you work we'll be breathing iodine.' He took a deep breath and turned to the little girl. 'You'll see how much fun we have, Princess.'

'Sara has to go to nursery school.'

'Don't be cruel.'

'Don't be cruel,' Fernando repeated, hugging the girl.

Luca and Pietro looked to each other. Then the doctor went back inside the building, returning with an additional duffel and without the schoolbag. 'OK, then.'

Sara ran to her father and danced around him, unable to contain herself for joy.

The lawyer waited in front of the van, holding the heads of two matches in his fist. 'And the winner is . . .' He held them out to Pietro.

The concierge came up with the shorter match. 'And so?'

'And so drive carefully, because I have a weak stomach.' He sat down in the front passenger seat.

Luca had Sara get in next to Paola. 'I'll be here behind you, honey.' And he sat down next to Fernando.

'Are we going to Mama's now?' murmured Sara.

Paola caressed her face. 'Did you know that the sea has dolphins that leap into the sky?'

The lawyer twisted around in his seat in front of them, pulled the peacock feather from the fur hat and handed it to the child. 'It's like your magic wand. Touch your nose three times and you'll see dolphins.'

Sara held the feather without doing anything further as Pietro started the van.

'Wait.' Paola opened her coat and drew out a small rosary made of coral. Stretched forward and tried to hang it from the rear-view mirror. 'The streets are dangerous.'

'You see, Pietro? She has more faith in God than in you.' Poppi pulled the rosary from her hands. 'She doesn't know that the Lord doesn't have a licence. Let's let the driver decide: do we keep the snake on the mirror or do we snuff it out?'

The concierge fastened his seat belt, released the hand brake and said, 'Let's keep it.'

The young priest and the witch approached the dance floor. The people said, 'That's the priest. That's the witch.' They ran to a dark corner of the beach, beneath ivy climbing between two huts. 'It's not music that moves your priest's feet.' She brought her ankles together and raised one leg to the side, held on to the ivy and spun in place. 'It's not what moves my witch's body, either.'

He slipped a rosary from his wrist and struck his heels

together, softly, harder, struck them in a tapping rhythm that challenged the heavens. 'It's fear of the Lord that moves them.'

The ivy shook above them and dropped what had hidden among the leaves, snail shells crusted with salt.

'It's fear.'

They came together. The young priest placed a hand on her belly. The witch said, 'I saw my son when he came into the world, he was small as these snails.'

His feet abruptly stopped, appeased by their kiss.

After half an hour on the motorway, the lawyer turned toward the passengers. Fernando was taking everyone's picture. Poppi produced a CD, slipped an index finger through the disc's hole and spun. Inserted it into the player and adjusted the volume, and the song began: *The sea in winter is just a black-and-white movie seen on TV*. Fernando took a picture of Luca dozing against the window with a hat pulled down over eyes that pretended to sleep. *And looking inland, clouds throw themselves down from the sky*. Took a picture of Paola as she told Sara a story about mermaids, of Sara as she touched her nose with her wishing feather and said, 'I want to be a mermaid who swims with the dolphins.' Took a picture of himself, of love for Alice still on his chubby face. *The sea, the sea, here no one ever comes to drag me away. The sea, the sea, here no one ever comes to keep us company*. The lawyer and Pietro went out of focus. The coral rosary on the mirror separated them while the song went on, *But then one evening, a strange concert on the beach, a single umbrella that stays open. Confused I plunge into moments lived once before*.

The Deluxe van approached the bridge over the Po River. Pietro accelerated and Paola said, 'Be careful.' He accelerated again and the rosary struck the windscreen. Passed two cars and they changed into the right lane. The guard rails had been broken through and patched up with temporary barriers. 'Oh my goodness.' She brought a hand to her mouth. 'Please slow down.'

Pietro stared at the hole in the guard rail as they sped past.

'Do you know the alphabet game?' the lawyer asked.

They climbed the bridge and no one answered. The river was in flood. A broken-down boat was crossing from one bank to the other.

'The sea!' Fernando pointed the camera at the window.

The little girl touched the feather to her nose three times.

'It's the river, dear. There aren't any dolphins in there.' Paola patted her head. 'What were you saying about the alphabet, Mr Poppi?'

'The winner is the one who recreates the alphabet from "a" to "z" with the first letters of the road signs. First "a", then "b", then "c" and so on. Just the first letters. Sara, the doctor and I will take the right side of the road, Pietro, Paola and Fernando, the left side. Make sense? Let's begin.'

'Viola,' exclaimed Fernando.

'What's "v" got to do with it?' Paola turned toward her son, followed by the other passengers. The boy was staring at the display of the mobile phone ringing in the doctor's hand.

They crossed to the far bank.

Without indicating, Pietro moved toward the shoulder

and Luca said into the phone, 'I'm on my way to Rimini. Sara is with me . . .'

Poppi motioned for Pietro to accelerate. Luca spluttered, 'We're only staying a few hours, then we'll be back.'

The Deluxe van continued on the shoulder until they came to a service area and Autogrill, where they parked.

'Second breakfasts for everyone.' The lawyer opened the sliding door.

Fernando jumped out first. 'Cappuccino.'

The last in the van were Luca and his daughter. He passed her the phone and she spoke into it, tapping a finger against the glass, then handed the phone to her father and got out.

Paola led her away. 'What did your mama say to you?'

The lawyer went up to Pietro. 'The love affairs of gays end more quickly even than yours, goodness knows, but you know what the real difference is? There aren't any children stuck in the middle. The uterus is the source of unhappiness, my friend.'

'The source of you as well, Mr Poppi.'

'Exactly.' He adjusted his fur hat and followed the others into the restaurant.

The concierge waited in the middle of the car park and checked his coat pockets. Felt the elephant. And the old man's recorder.

Luca caught up with him. 'She wants to talk to me as soon as I get back.'

# 37

They left the motorway and the last letter of the alphabet game was 'm'. The lawyer read at the top of his voice, *Marvel at the Grand Hotel,* on a billboard right before the toll booth for North Rimini. 'We're "m", you're "g", we win.' Poppi spread his arms. 'And now, let's marvel at this Grand Hotel, selected by my credit card.'

'I want to return this evening,' said Luca.

'It will do us good,' the lawyer said to the group. Then again, more softly, to the doctor, 'It will do us good.'

Fernando raised his hand. Sara imitated him and Paola, blushing, also raised a finger.

'Four against two. And anyway, I've already made the reservation. Three suites, room service at breakfast, and sea views included. It's my treat. I'm only taking receipts to the grave.'

The concierge pulled the van over. 'Where are we going, Doctor?'

'Everyone to the Grand Hotel,' replied the lawyer.

'Where, Doctor?'

'Where they want to go, Pietro. I don't want any revolts.'

The van rejoiced. The concierge sat frozen with the engine running, the coral rosary swinging from the mirror.

'Let's go,' said Poppi.

The van stayed still.

'What is it, Pietro?' Paola laid a hand on his shoulder.

The concierge put the vehicle in gear and they set off, slowly at first. He followed a trunk road for a bit, then they came to a roundabout where he slowed almost to a stop, turned into the road that cuts across the city and leads to the sea. Rimini was desolate, grey in the cold, grey also on account of the abandonment resort towns permit themselves in the autumn. Luca lowered his window. The salty air entered and Pietro coughed, pressed his nose against his sleeve as they drove around the ramparts and past the Tiberius Bridge. They skirted the harbour and came to a boulevard with a string of villas. At the end was a piazza, at the centre of which stood a fountain with four stone horses blowing water from their nostrils.

'They've got a cold,' Fernando said, pointing.

The concierge kept his eyes on the steering wheel and the others said that it would be worth it to get out, it really would. He continued on to a panoramic terrace with a giant camera sculpture in the middle and parked nearby. Paola said, 'There's the sea.'

There was the sea. Without the waves. Without the beach umbrellas. The sand tracked out with old footprints. Further on, the lighthouse was silent.

'Everyone out,' the lawyer said.

They emerged one by one. Luca picked up the little girl and crossed the pavement in one long step. The lawyer took off his shoes and socks. Fernando did the same and Paola said to him, 'You'll be sick later, put your shoes back on.'

Fernando took a picture of her and didn't put his shoes back on, instead he ran for the shore. Pietro set off as well, his nose pressed to a handkerchief. He followed in the footsteps of his son as far as the shuttered concession stand with its tin-plate ice-cream menus.

Paola caught up with him there. 'How is it to come back?'

'I've never left.' Pietro removed his nose from the handkerchief and the air burned in his lungs. He passed the stand and walked along the beach, the sand climbing his legs. He advanced and Paola followed, went toward the sea, closer and closer till he came to the water's edge. There was a band of broken shells, which Fernando and the lawyer picked from. The concierge stopped and the water touched his shoes, *I will protect you, my son.* Touched Paola's shoes, *Make Pietro fall in love with me.* Washed over the bare feet of the lawyer, *This is my family.* And those of Fernando, *Are you at the bottom of the sea, Papa?* Kissed the shoes of the doctor, *What am I going to do?*

The water receded, and Luca said to Pietro, 'We have to go.'

Sara said goodbye to her father as she touched the feather to her nose.

'What did you wish for, honey?'

She spoke under her breath. 'That you come back soon.'

'I won't be long. You'll have more fun with the others.'

'That you come back soon to our house,' she said more loudly.

He entrusted the little girl to Paola and continued with Pietro along the beach. They went back up to the promenade at the fourth beach. A group of tourists stood gazing upwards: the Grand Hotel was an ivory cathedral.

'Let's take the van,' said the concierge as he pulled out the keys. The doctor didn't reply and continued on foot. Passed into the pedestrian area that led back to the fountain of the four horses. The water roared like they were already there. The concierge caught up with him at the entrance to the piazza. 'Where is the appointment?'

'This fountain is strange.'

Pietro pointed to the pine grove just beyond. 'In there in the summer, there's a course with tricycles shaped like animals. The priests from the seminary would take me there.'

Luca took a coin from his pocket. 'It's a fountain for lovers.'

'For tourists.'

'For lovers, my mother used to say. But she always was the sentimental type.' He tossed the coin into the water, making the same wish his daughter had.

They went along the boulevard with the string of villas to each side and took the passageway beneath the station. They came out on to a cobbled street that led to a piazza with a glass dome over the remains of a Roman *domus*, where they stopped.

Pietro looked down at the cobblestones. 'How do they manage to contact you to schedule a visit?'

'They turn to organizations for the terminally ill.' He shook the leather bag. 'There are also exceptional cases.'

'The old man from the petrol station's son.'

'The old man, not his son. If I agree to do it, he'll take Andrea with him. If I agree this time, I'll be taking a risk.'

They stood close, shoes brushing. 'Why do you do it?'

The doctor was silent, moved away slightly. 'Their eyes. It's enough to look them in the eyes.' He moved a bit further away. When he reached the edge of the piazza he raised his face to the plaque with its name.

Pietro, too, raised his face to the plaque. 'There isn't any patient in Rimini, is there?'

A pale mist floated in from the sea, brining the air and obscuring the walls of the houses. Father and son came together, remained one against the other in the piazza that preserved the past. Then Luca asked Pietro to follow him.

'I'm stopping here.' The concierge pulled back.

'When my mother was dying she told me that she had had one single passion in life. "Papa," I said to her. "No," she said.'

'I'm stopping here.'

'"It was someone I knew before I was married," my mother said. "The only good secret in my life. The others are all horrible or dull or only known to the Lord."'

'You should stop here as well, Luca.'

'"It was the end of a summer by the sea. It all started with a cat and a bicycle."' The doctor's face surfaced in the mist. At the far end of the piazza stood the eighteenth-century church, beside it a two-storey house with closed shutters. The facade had recently been repainted, dark green rather than yellow.

Luca went closer to Pietro again. 'I asked my mother how she came to marry my father. She said, "Papa was the love for a lifetime." So what was the other? "The other was the love of a lifetime."' The doctor pressed the hair down at his neck. 'And do you know what my mother said when I wanted to know why her love of a lifetime ended?'

Pietro looked at him. Luca was a silhouette cut into the white.

'My mother said: "It takes courage to tear a lover away from the Lord. And I've always been a big chicken."' Luca looked toward the far end of the piazza. 'She also said something about me: she said that I was what held her and my father together. She admitted that having a child together had strengthened the relationship.' He stopped. 'Was that the church, Pietro?'

He made no reply.

And the doctor continued: 'I knew that my mother had spent her holidays in Rimini until she was twenty-five. When I heard where you were from and that you had been a priest I thought you could have been that someone.'

'What else did she tell you?'

'Nothing else.' He began to walk. 'What else should she have said?'

'Yes, that's the church.'

The mist lifted and Luca said, 'Tell me what the love of a lifetime is like, Pietro.'

'Why?'

'Because I've just lost it.'

Pietro left the centre of the piazza, skirted the Roman *domus* and stopped under the portico in front of the church.

The doctor approached him. 'You met her here?'

A middle-aged priest came out of the house and hastened to open the church. Pietro stayed behind a column of the portico.

'Don Paolo,' called a man who was passing, 'last night I dreamt about God.'

'How was He?'

'A bit tired,' he laughed. 'He told me there is something after we're dead and we'll all find each other there.' The man said goodbye and turned the corner.

The middle-aged priest nodded and before returning inside said, 'Of course, if there's nothing, we've really been cheated.'

Pietro took a step forward and squatted down, rested a hand where the cat had been struck by the witch, picked up a bunch of dry leaves. They crumbled in his hand. 'Is this enough for you, Doctor?'

Luca shook his head. 'Why did you seek each other out after so much time?'

'You want to know?'

The doctor nodded. Pietro stood up and let the leaves fall. 'No one ever told me I'd find her again after I'm dead.'

# 38

The mist became fog as father and son arrived at the house of the witch. It had smooth walls now but the plaster already looked patchy. An old woman sat in the front garden, her ankles obscured by the leaves of a fig tree. Pietro tipped his hat and she murmured, 'I remember you. Give my best to the Lord!'

They walked around the fenced-in courtyard. At the back was a small summerhouse, through whose window they could see the poster of a singer and a boxy chandelier. 'Let's get back to the others,' Pietro said.

'This was my mother's house?'

'Let's get back to the others.'

They returned down the street towards the sea. Luca called Poppi and the lawyer's voice blared from the phone, 'Come quickly, the dolphins have chosen Fernando!'

'They're at the Dolphinarium.'

The concierge smiled.

'Did you know that it was Poppi who wanted you at any cost?'

He nodded.

'There were thirteen of you. All with experience except you and two others. The lawyer insisted with the other owners. "He's got the right vibrations," he said.'

'The right vibrations.'

'He would have done anything for my mother. They were great friends.'

The lighthouse sounded for the first time and they went to meet the echo of the past. Found themselves in front of the anchor monument at the beginning of the breakwater. Along the left side ran a quay where tied-up fishing boats slipped slowly back and forth. The lighthouse sounded again and Pietro plugged his ears. They crossed the street towards the Dolphinarium, a concrete cylinder dividing the open sand from the first official beach. There was no one queuing. Pietro bought two tickets and as soon as Luca joined him said, 'They're waiting for us.'

Only Paola was waiting for them. She was the only one seated around the dolphin tank with her face turned toward the entrance. She held Sara's feet between her knees while the little girl leaned on the tank wall and flailed her arms. The lawyer was running to and fro and taking pictures.

Fernando was in a dinghy towed by a dolphin, his glasses slipped to the end of his nose and his beret hanging to one side. Two dolphins leapt over him, spraying him with water, and he fixed his hat. He peered out at the crowd, fearful, looking for his mother. Waved to her and Sara and waved to the audience, then a man in diving gear took the microphone and said, 'A round of applause for Fernando, a round of applause.' The few people applauded. Paola gripped the little girl's ankles. Gripped more tightly and from beneath her sunglasses came two rivulets.

'A final round of applause for Fernando!'

The strange boy finished his ride, then was led to choose a

fish from a bucket. This he brought to one of the dolphins waiting at the edge of the tank. The animal tore it from his fingers and Fernando leapt backwards in fright. The man in the diving gear gave him a souvenir tied with ribbons and told him he could return to his friends.

'He's coming, Paola.' Pietro helped her to stand.

She wiped her face, opened her arms and ran toward Fernando. The lawyer took a picture of the mother with the half smile and the son who pulled away.

The music from the dance floor stopped and the fog consumed that tiny square of sand as well. Someone said it was time to go home. Someone else had already gone home. Everyone had forgotten the witch and the priest, hidden by the ivy between the huts.

'My son was as small as this.' She knelt down and picked up a snail shell. 'I buried him under a tree. The next day I went back and the tree had lost all its leaves.' The witch slipped off one shoulder strap and then another. The fog entered the ivy and the dress fell.

The lawyer gave out the room assignments. Fernando protested when he found out that he would be sleeping with his mother. Asked to stay with Pietro, pulling him into a hug. The strange boy cooled down as soon as he saw one of the bartenders at the Grand Hotel, raven-haired and with braids pinned up on the crown of her head. She greeted him. 'Would you like something to drink, sir?' He sat down at the bar. 'Is your name Alice?'

The doctor collected his keys and went straight upstairs with his daughter to room 316. When they entered Sara shrank down in amazement. There were beautiful flowers on the bedside table and star-shaped chocolates on the bed, a bowl of fruit wrapped in a red ribbon, golden chairs and the sea just out of the window. She explored the room on legs like pogo sticks, disappeared into the bathroom and reappeared on the balcony, a friendly little phantom bursting out of her skin.

To the concierge went the lawyer in 318. And the latter immediately set things straight. 'Now don't get any ideas. I'm no easy conquest.' Poppi opened one of his suitcases. 'It took my Daniele two days.' Winked and collapsed into an armchair. 'And a lifetime wasn't enough for him to leave me. These days love affairs are dropping like flies, just look at Luca and Madame.'

'The doctor knew about her and the other man.'

'Good God, even Fernando and his cactus knew. Luca suffers from vertigo but he's someone who jumps. And then he's always known what his wife is like.'

'What is she like?'

'Viola? Beauty, she's got. A brain and a sense of irony, ditto. Sensuality, she's got in spades, but reliability? That depends.'

'On what?'

'On her desire to reproduce, my friend. And on what there is on the horizon. Faster flies, more stable ones.'

'She's different than she appears. She's just fragile.'

'She's - different - than - she - appears - she's - just - fragile.' He snorted. 'You could write for the theatre, Pietro. Or become a priest. Think about it . . .' He rested his feet on the table. 'The woman could be exactly what she appears.'

The mirror on the wall reflected the two four-poster beds and the bouquet of hydrangeas on the coffee table. It reflected the concierge, his chin bowed low on his breast. 'Tell me what you know about the two of them.'

Poppi examined the bowl of fruit served with best wishes from the Grand Hotel. 'A woman would kill to be a mother.' He hesitated over an apple. 'They tried to have one for years. I heard the desperation every month when they came up empty.'

'What do you know?'

'For me the child will always be Luca's daughter and no one else's. The bond is what counts, not the testicles.' He selected a cluster of grapes and lowered it into his mouth.

Pietro looked outside. The sea was a sheet of steel under the last rays of the sun. 'Tell me what you know . . .' – he turned – 'what you know about me.'

Poppi put down the cluster of grapes, went to the sliding glass door and opened it. 'That you're a very absent-minded concierge who doesn't like cats, but a more than observant man.'

'What else?' He followed him onto the balcony.

'I'm a poof, Pietro. And hysterical. I'm alone and speak with a forked tongue. But there's one thing, my friend, that I'll never do: reveal the secrets of a lifetime.'

'Celeste.'

'Celeste asked me to send you a letter and to keep you in consideration if you applied. Full stop. Celeste told me that you were a man to depend on, a man with tap-dancing in his past.' He smoothed his eyebrows with his thumb. 'The rest I understood on my own. You, Pietro, know what it means to live on the memory of the one you love.'

'At a certain point that comes to an end as well.'

The lights went on along the promenade. From the beach, a group of old men and women pointed offshore to a cruise liner lit up from bow to stern. The fog descended again and voices in the group said it was the *Rex*, the *Rex*. The lawyer went back in and rummaged in one of his bags, fished out a suit wrapped in cellophane. 'For you, Pietro. You're too *charmant* not to merit a bit of blue.' Poppi removed his turtleneck, his shoes and trousers. Beat his fists against his ribs. 'This is the flesh that separates me from my Daniele?'

The concierge looked closely at the bones pushing through the skin. 'All you have to do is wait.'

'To die?' The lawyer headed to the bathroom. 'I've always been bored waiting.' He opened the door. 'Do you know the poet Prévert? A smooth-tongued fellow with a brain: *Les feuilles mortes se ramassent à la pelle, les souvenirs et les regrets aussi*. Dead leaves are collected by the shovelful, memories and regrets as well.' As he shut himself inside: 'I'm buried in them up to my neck.'

The fog entered 318 and Pietro saw no longer. He rested a hand on his ribs, tapped.

Celeste held the snail in one palm with the dress at her ankles and caressed Pietro's hands that only knew how to pray.

Helped him to remove his sweater, his shirt. The light from the lighthouse returned and she saw the bruises on his ribs.

Pietro searched his pockets, pulled out a stone rosary and fastened it to his wrist, a strangling snake. 'I don't know how to swim very well.' Stepped out of his trousers.

'It's because you carry weights around.' She fingered the rosary and finished undressing him, drew him out from beneath the ivy.

They ran naked as far as the water's edge then scrambled up on the rocks flanking the jetty. Pietro held a hand over his sex and looked at the witch's ballerina ankles.

They leapt. The water swirled and swallowed her, swirled and swallowed him. Enveloped feet, legs, necks. Celeste held the snail on the surface of the water. 'Forgive me, my child.' Released the snail and followed it beneath the water. Pietro turned in every direction, felt the witch moving below. He waited, and as he did so unfastened the rosary.

Pietro put on the lawyer's gift and saw that it fit him perfectly. Poppi sang in the shower the Loredana Bertè song he'd played them in the van. The concierge was in blue for the first time in his life. In the mirror he saw how he now matched Mastroianni in both the lines in his forehead and the tailor-made jacket. Pietro buttoned up the jacket and took Anita's jar out of the backpack. Took the recorder as well and put it in his pocket. *My name is Andrea Testi. I am thirty-four years old and I know how to dribble.* He left suite 318 and the Grand Hotel. The promenade was awash in fog. The electric signs for the various beaches were smoking. He could see the pale yellow of the street lamps and the red tail lamp of a bicycle that passed near him. Pietro had not been on the jetty since a night thirty-five years ago. He followed the promenade past the Dolphinarium with its shuttered ticket office, past the anchor monument. On the other side of the port, the dance floor had become a harbour for luxury vessels. The only music came from the low crashing of the waves. He rested on the wall that ran along the first stretch of the quay with the fishing boats, separating it from the sand. On the other side was an inlet. He climbed down and approached this narrow arm of the sea. Knelt and removed the lid from the jar, filled it with handfuls of frigid sand, filled it as Anita had asked him, a little at a time. Closed the jar and warmed it between his hands, protected. Held it like that as he turned around, passed the anchor again on his way to the end of the jetty.

Then and there he raised his eyes. The water was swelling. It swelled and he went to meet it. Climbed up onto the first rock, onto the second. Climbed down onto the third, and the water submerged the blue trousers up to his ankles. He stamped his feet once. The fog covered him and in the whiteness he began with the heel, continued with the toe.

# 39

Pietro returned along with the breeze that dissolved the fog and collected the leaves. That strewed dead dry leaves over the beach and the gardens of the Grand Hotel. Inside the main hall two musicians in livery were at the double bass and the violin. A pianist played with his hair dishevelled by the draught coming in at the door. The hall was crowded. Pietro saw them at the first table. Paola held a glass of wine in her hand, her gaze on her son seated at the bar. Fernando was dressed up. Every so often he would lean over on the bar stool and adjust his jacket without ever taking his eyes off the bartender.

'The best always arrive first – fashions have changed.' The lawyer came to meet him in a dinner jacket, bowed and noticed Pietro's trousers, wet to the ankles, and the jar of sand. 'One day you'll have to tell me what you do in your spare time.' Then he whispered in his ear: 'Ask Paola to dance. She's been dying for it all evening.' He led him to the table, in the middle of which stood a card with the crest of the Grand Hotel and the words 'Reserved for Deluxe Vans'. Luca sat apart from the others and dandled his daughter on his knees. Sara noticed the concierge and held up the plastic dolphin that Fernando had given her after his trip in the dinghy. The entire time, Luca did not turn his head.

'Update on our doctor . . .' The lawyer drained a flute of

champagne. 'Instead of Madame, Riccardo called him, but he wouldn't answer. Shall we dance?'

'No.'

'Come.' He took the jar from his hands and set it on the table, dragged the concierge onto the dance floor, held him as if to begin a waltz. Pietro tried to move away but soon gave up and allowed himself to be led. Poppi waltzed him once around the floor, then nodded to Paola.

She rose to her feet, her long dress trailing along the ground and barely covering her withered breasts. She came closer, a mass of curls atop her head, came closer still. Pietro found her in his arms in place of the lawyer. Paola clutched him with cold hands, the odour of face powder rising from her wizened face, yanked him into a turn. 'It's very easy, follow me.' She led him according to the notes played by the dishevelled pianist. 'Follow me.' Pietro followed her, watching past the curls as Fernando got down from his bar stool and went over to a vase of flowers at reception. Paola laid her cheek against the concierge's, breathed in deeply and said, 'See how easy it is, it's all a question of mutual understanding.' Fernando lifted a rose from the vase at reception and returned to the bar while his mother whispered in Pietro's ear, 'And there's no shortage of understanding between us.' Paola caressed the back of his neck. Her son attempted to do the same to the raven-haired bartender but she stepped aside with a smile. Paola smiled as well, 'I feel so safe here with you,' extended her lips to his neck. Fernando climbed over the bar, 'I want to marry you, Alice,' and the bartender backed away. The boy pushed his glasses up and held out the rose: 'You're my sweetheart.' A waiter stepped between them and pushed Fernando back. The boy persisted, crying, 'Alice, Alice,' as the mother was saying to Pietro, 'It's beautiful to grow old together, Pietro. There are so many things that we can do, you and I.' Fernando faced up to the waiter and swung the rose at him, slipped away and went after the girl. Caused her to fall, tumbling as well in the process and upturning a shelf of bottles onto himself. The concierge turned toward the bar. Everyone turned toward the bar except for Luca, who passed Sara to the lawyer and rushed up the stairs.

The pianist paused, smoothed back his ruffled hair and told the other musicians that they must distract the guests. He began to play but no one was distracted from the strange boy being subdued by two waiters.

Pietro left the dance floor when Fernando was already back on his feet and being attended to by Paola. He reached the stairs and climbed to their floor. The windows on the corridor were all wide open. Sand floated in on the wind. Luca was at the far end on the phone, saying, 'Everything's fine, Sara's fine. What did you want to tell me today? Tell me now, tell me for God's sake. I said, tell me. What does it matter, tomorrow or now?' He leaned out over the windowsill and the wind ruffled his hair. 'Tell me,' he shouted into the phone. 'I don't want to be told in person, I want to be told now, hello? Viola? Hello, hello?' He brought the mobile away from his ear, looked at it, dropped it to the carpet and noticed the concierge. Ran a hand over his hair and covered his face. 'Would I look out of that window to fall in love again?' he asked in a thread of a voice.

'You would.'

'For my daughter?'

'For what you've become.'

Luca picked up the mobile and slid it over the sill to him. 'A doctor who competes for souls with God? What else?'

Pietro drew out the old man's recorder and handed it to him. 'A father.'

The rosary sank down and settled into the sand. Celeste was also swimming along the bottom. Pietro felt her near his legs, twitched. She stroked his feet and came up. She placed her hands on his scarred ribs and said, 'What we're doing is just a form of prayer.' She wrapped her legs around him. 'Our prayer.'

Pietro stopped twitching and looked at her. Witches have Milanese accents and frightened eyes that are more beautiful still. He stared at the sky, then filled his hands with what they had never before touched, sought her glorious breasts, her thighs, her legs and worked back up.

Celeste stopped his hands at her stomach. Their prayer began when he entered her.

The doctor returned to the main hall of the Grand Hotel. Pietro stood at the window. The cruise liner illuminated a slice of sea. At the end of the jetty the lighthouse was dark. The only light remaining was the glow of a restaurant on stilts.

'Luca told me you were here.'

Pietro turned around. Paola advanced awkwardly in her high heels, faltered. Her cheeks were plastered with make-up and her lips dry at the corners.

'How is Fernando?'

She leaned her head on his shoulder, her breath smelling of wine. 'He's with Poppi.' Hugged him close. The piano downstairs started up and Paola took a deep breath. 'I don't know what to do with him.' Hugged him closer. 'I never have.'

The lights of the restaurant on stilts went out as well.

Paola tugged at the hem of his jacket. 'Come with me to get Fernando's pills?'

'I'll wait for you here.'

She found the keys in her handbag, took him by the hand and dragged him to room 314. Opened the door and pulled him inside, pushing the door not quite closed. Rested her forehead on his chin as if they were still dancing.

The concierge held her up. 'The others are waiting for us.' He tried to lead her out but Paola pushed his hands aside. She took a deep breath and knelt down. Unzipped his trousers and burrowed a hand inside. Pietro backed away but she was quicker, taking his sex into her mouth. She kept on, mascara streaking down her cheeks, kept on until Pietro pushed her face away. 'The others are waiting for us.'

She collapsed backward, spread her arms out on the carpet and remained still. The concierge pulled her up, Paola burbling. As he laid her out on the bed a bustling came from the corridor, then a knock. The lawyer entered with Fernando clinging to his neck. The boy's glasses were askew and he had a sticking plaster on one temple.

'One and one makes two, the complete set,' he said upon seeing the wine-addled woman. Arranged the boy beside his mother and kissed him on the forehead, went out.

The concierge followed him into the corridor. 'It must be the iodine.'

Poppi took his arm. 'I always knew you had a sense of humour down there somewhere.'

# 40

Pietro slept in room 318, his face peeking out above a sheet pulled up to his chin. His legs were drawn up to one side and he snored faintly. The night before as he climbed into bed he managed to hear Poppi: 'Goodnight, dear friend, and thanks.'

The concierge fell asleep immediately after that. The lawyer never did. His hands were folded over his silk dressing gown, his cheeks whitened by anti-wrinkle cream. He had stayed in bed, motionless, and then all of a sudden murmured, 'Mazel tov,' then nothing again for the rest of the night.

In the middle of the night Poppi gritted his teeth, sighed, pulled his hands outside the sheets and brought them to his nose. For once he was not afraid, just ashamed. The old man slowly rose to his feet. Unbuttoned the pyjama top to discover the bottoms wet with urine. Closed himself in the bathroom as Pietro opened his eyes and looked to the windows. The *chooo* of the lighthouse had returned. Fernando opened his eyes as well in room 314. His mother put her arms around him and the boy tried to free himself from that embrace that seemed to come from a wife rather than a mother. *Chooo*, the lighthouse blew, and the last to hear it was Luca in room 316. He woke abruptly, the bundle of Sara pressed up against his side. She slept, still. He drew her hair away from her face. Pulled himself up and went to the French doors. Rimini in the winter is a great lady. His jacket hung from the coat rack. He searched in one pocket, then another, found the recorder and went out onto the balcony. Turned it on. The lighthouse started up again. Beneath that blast of sound each of them discovered the courage they had never before had.

'My name is Andrea Testi. I am thirty-four years old and I know how to dribble. You have to have strong ankles to dribble well, and I have strong ankles. But what really counts is your eye. Look straight at your opponent, straight at him. Then ankle, ball, ankle. I can dribble right past people. I want to do it again. Ask Daniele Bucchi how I dribble, he's my captain, a real bear of a defender. When you've got the ball and he comes at you, he takes it off everyone but yours truly. In training, I swear, he's never taken the ball off me. I'd say to him, "I dare you," and he'd say, "Look out." He has never once taken the ball off me. Daniele Bucchi says I'll be coming back to dribble him again, and that he's training twice as hard for when I get up from the wheelchair and return to the field. The captain is always talking bullshit. After the wheelchair I'm headed for the bed. It's written on my chart at the hospital. It also says I won't speak any more. If that's the way it goes, God's lucky he's not a defender. If that's the way it goes, ankle, ball, ankle. Look straight at your opponent. Better to snuff it. I say it and this is my voice. My name is Andrea Testi and I know how to dribble. I swear, it's better to snuff it.'

# 41

The lawyer's team won. When they were still on the motorway he came to the end of the alphabet with the 'z' on a billboard for Zapis Thermal Baths. Poppi played alone. Paola stared out of the window with a scarf over her head and knotted under her chin. Fernando was in a virtual trance the entire trip. No one from Pietro's team had been up for it. Luca travelled with his daughter on his knees: 'Did you like the dolphins, honey?' She nodded. 'Will you take me on the dinghy?'

Pietro watched them in the rear-view mirror. The rosary swung when they sped down the bridge over the River Po. In the other direction the guard rail was still broken. Paola pointed it out. Fernando closed the case with his camera inside. The last picture snapped was of Alice at the Grand Hotel whose name was actually Nicole and whose boyfriend was a lifeguard in the summer and a night-club DJ in the winter. She had winked at Fernando and he had taken her picture. *You're my sweetheart – Me? Sorry, I've already got a sweetheart.*

Luca's mobile rang as they came to the end of the bridge. It had rung as soon as they left Rimini, then twice more, and he had not answered. He did so when they reached the toll booth for Milan. 'Come by tomorrow morning at nine-thirty and tell me what you have to say. I'll take Sara to nursery school.'

The little girl stared at her father and tapped her nose with the feather. She dropped it when they arrived at the studio flat. Got out and fluttered three fingers to say goodbye. Fernando reciprocated with three fingers at the window.

'It breaks my heart to see the doctor like this.' Paola unwound the rosary from the rear-view mirror and gave it to the concierge. 'You keep it, it will make me happy.'

Pietro put the rosary in his pocket and before they arrived home fastened it to his wrist. He had to park right next to the tram stop. The petrol-blue SUV took up the two spaces near the street door.

'Golden curls doesn't waste any time.' The lawyer pointed to Riccardo, who was struggling to unload a shopping bag from the luggage compartment. His right leg was in a cast up to his knee that visibly threw him off balance. 'How sorry I am,' Poppi sniggered. 'He's hurt himself, the poor lion.'

No one got out of the van.

'She's there as well,' said Paola.

Viola could be seen at the entrance, holding more bags.

'Everyone out.'

Fernando was the first. He gathered up their bags and went in without saying goodbye. Paola was the last. After the lawyer got out she spoke with the scarf over her mouth. 'I'm sorry about last night, Pietro.'

'Can I take Fernando out tonight?'

'Him?'

'Him.'

Paola sighed. 'If he's not tired. I'll let you know.'

The concierge returned the keys to the lawyer and went over to Riccardo, picked up the remaining shopping bag.

It was filled to the brim with stuffed animals. He also spotted a pair of children's pyjamas, a bathrobe and towel set. 'What happened to your leg?'

'Five-a-side football isn't made for someone almost forty.'

The concierge closed the SUV. 'I'll come up with you.'

They climbed the stairs together, Riccardo relying on his crutches. After the first flight he leaned on the concierge's shoulder. 'How was it going back to the sea?'

'A bit of fresh air for everyone.'

'Including Luca?'

Pietro helped him start up again. 'Let's go.' Supported him all the way up to the second floor.

Viola stood on the threshold. 'Pietro.'

Riccardo pretended to swipe at her with a crutch. 'If it weren't for him . . .' He smiled.

'I was on my way.' She had the concierge hand her the bag. 'Please come in, both of you.'

'I need to go, I forgot my prescription pad at the office.' Riccardo started off and Viola followed him. 'You're going *how?*'

'I'll take a taxi.'

She waved goodbye uncertainly, then invited Pietro inside. 'I'll make you a coffee.'

'I already had two at the Autogrill,' he replied as he followed her in. They stopped in the living room, where he looked at her. Her hair was recently cut, layered toward the bottom, her face gaunt. She nibbled at her lips and crossed her arms, pushing her breasts forward. 'Did you have a good time at the sea?'

'We took Sara to the Dolphinarium. She had fun.'

Viola, not knowing where to look, stared at a slice of the couch. The polka-dot gloves were balled up between a cushion and the seat back. She picked them up and smoothed them between her hands, twice, before laying them on an end table. 'I know what you're thinking, Pietro.'

'What am I thinking?' He looked for the photograph of the lavender field but it was gone, replaced by a pale rectangle.

'That I'm throwing everything away.'

'All Luca needs is the child,' he said point-blank.

Viola motioned for him to sit down. 'It's more complicated than that.'

He did not sit. Found the lavender photograph behind the door, atop a pile of cardboard boxes. Pointed to it. 'What's left of that?'

Viola continued to stare at the gloves. The wrinkle persisted. She smoothed them out once more. 'At a certain point I stopped loving him.' Then she touched a pocket of her jeans.

'What's left of that?' He pointed at the lavender.

Viola once again brought a hand to her pocket. 'In the end they're just things, Pietro.' She pulled out a mobile that was vibrating. Read the message. 'I knew it' – she held her breath – 'Riccardo is going over to Luca's.'

Pietro and Celeste remained one inside the other and he ceased to gasp. She continued to gasp and her legs were no longer those of a ballerina.

'They're shaking.' Celeste ran her fingers lightly over the bruises on his chest. 'My legs are shaking because God is offended.' Drew herself away from him and disappeared underwater, resurfacing with the beads. 'Mama says that God is in things.' Handed him the rosary.

Pietro refused it. 'Mine aren't shaking any more.'

Viola left the flat with Pietro. 'Riccardo is capable of waiting for him all night if I don't take him away.' She pulled out the keys to the SUV. 'Did Luca tell you where he was going?'

He said no and she hurried down the stairs.

Pietro stopped on the landing. The lawyer's door was open partway and through the crack Poppi was staring at him, his skull pale in the half-light. He wore a mild smile and had a hand open in an ageless gesture of farewell. Pietro reciprocated and took two steps down. Turned around again and the lawyer was no longer there.

The concierge continued down and went into the lodge. Picked up the telephone and dialled the doctor's mobile number. He was not available at this time. He called Anita. He told her that that evening he would bring her the little something from Rimini, and that he had a big favour to ask her. Hung up and went to get the Bianchi. It had a layer of dust on the top bar. He wheeled it out.

Pietro had guessed right. He found Luca on the ward speaking to two nurses and carrying Sara. 'She's really grown,' said one. Sara remained motionless, captivated by a little boy playing in the room beyond a glass door. He was bent over a plastic table and searching for a puzzle piece to continue forming the image of an elk.

The doctor said something to his daughter and she nodded. He put her down and they led her into the room with the little boy. When Pietro approached, Luca went over to him. 'What's happened?'

'They're looking for you at your place.'

Sara had sat down near the little boy and was searching for pieces to the puzzle. The nurses were helping. The elk was missing the tips of its antlers and its nose.

'Looking for me at my place.' He sighed. 'Do you see the little boy with Sara? His name is Davide and he's obsessed with tractors and cement mixers. And especially with those lorries with two trailers. His life hangs in the balance, like Lorenzo's.' He moved aside for Pietro. 'If you look at him closely, you'll see that he's a happy child, even if he's guessed the end is coming.'

Davide picked up a piece and fitted it into the puzzle.

'Sara's life, on the other hand, doesn't hang in the balance. Instead of cement mixers she likes magic tricks. And now dolphins. But she too has guessed that an end is coming, her family's. If you look at her closely, you'll see that she'll never be truly happy again.' Luca laid a hand on the glass door. 'In some way they're both my children.'

'I know.'

'Sara arrived by a miracle. They call it asthenozoospermia, lazy sperm. I have the balls to dole out death – less so for life.'

Davide found the missing piece. Tried to insert it into the

puzzle. Sara came to his aid and the elk's antlers gained their tips.

'They're looking for you.'

'They agreed to tomorrow morning at nine-thirty.' Luca opened the glass door. 'Whatever they want will be less important than this.'

# 42

When Pietro returned from the hospital he realized that the lodge was a mess. The backed-up post had spilled onto the table and a thick layer of dust covered the floor. There were marks on the tiles from the Bianchi's tyres, continuing inside the flat. The courtyard, too, was filling up with rubbish. The plants had yellowed and dead leaves blocked the gutters. The Madonna's face was still sooty black. The pedestal was buried in snail shells, which also covered the ground below the alcove.

He began with the lodge. Distributed the post that had arrived on the Rimini days, set aside anything addressed to Luca and swept all the muck into a corner. Into the condominium's dustbin went the empty shells and the dead leaves from the courtyard. Next came the plants. He pulled up the dying ones from their pots, sparing only two, a thriving ficus and a recovering reed that he transplanted to the sliver of earth running along the hedge. Moved on to the lodge window, dotted with fingerprints. Steamed the glass with his breath and cleaned it with a piece of cotton cloth, making little circles of hot breath and wiping them smoothly away, again and again, until he could see himself in pristine reflection. Refilled the bucket with lukewarm water and ammonia. The cloth was already inside. Starting with the fourth floor he polished the stairs and the landings. When he reached the second floor he heard that Viola and Riccardo had returned. Continued on down to the first floor, then into the entrance hall, into the lodge and finally did the floor of his own flat. The marks from the Bianchi only came away after great effort. The floor tiles in the bedroom, he had never before touched. They were filthy and larded with plaster drippings. He swapped the putrid water for boiling water and knelt down. Plunged his hands into the cloth. *We've got ourselves a boy on the ball.* Began to scrub, scrubbed with hands ridged with tendons. *He's our son.* Scraped, relentlessly pressed down until the filth began to dissolve. Travelled the circuit of the room on all fours, pulling away the pustules of plaster. His knees reddened. He didn't stop. The pungent ammonia rose into and swelled his eyes. He dried them against his shoulder and paused to breathe, then began again. Bent over like this, he was a small man made smaller. Exhausted, he scoured the last tiles nearly unable to draw breath. Came to the suitcase. Set it aside and cleaned the eight tiles on which it rested. *He's our son.* Removed the boxes, all the boxes, from the suitcase, and when he finished he closed it. Fastened the latches, first one, then the other. Paused to look at it. *I'll protect him, Celeste, I promise you.*

Pietro rose to stand with the cloth dripping black and tossed it into the bucket, into water equally dark.

He went to pour it into the bathroom sink and stripped. His arms were shaking and his skin glistened with sweat. He was soaked. He got into the shower and emptied the shampoo bottle, scrubbed his head like the tiles. Rinsed himself off. Directly he finished drying off he put on his white shirt and the brogues, knotted his tie. Then the jacket. *I'll protect him.* Finally the backpack with Anita's jar. *I promise you.*

Pietro went back up to the second floor. From the lawyer's flat came the murmur of the television and from the Martinis' the voice of Viola. He rang the doorbell at Fernando's.

Paola opened immediately.

'You didn't let me know anything,' said Pietro.

'You've got to see how elegant he looks.' She scuffed her shoe on the doormat and urged her son to show himself.

Fernando came out onto the landing in vicuña trousers and a white shirt, his beret and a duffel coat one size too big. Touched the sticking plaster at his temple. 'Trip with Pietro.'

'We'll be back soon.'

Paola adjusted her son's coat. 'Have fun. I'm going to hole up with the lawyer for some Buraco.' She kissed him. 'How are you going?'

'In a taxi.' Pietro waved goodbye and led Fernando by the hand down into the entrance hall. The Bianchi was leaning against the downpipe, sparkling.

'In a taxi.' Fernando pointed to it and laughed.

Once in the street Pietro climbed onto the saddle and helped the strange boy to sit sideways on the top tube. Perching there with difficulty, he entrusted himself to Pietro, twisting down and forward and grasping the handlebars. They took off immediately. Fernando brought one hand to his beret, which threatened to fly away. His rear end began to hurt as soon as the Bianchi started over the cobblestones. Then the road smoothed out. 'Go fast,' he said, and the Bianchi sailed between two cars and through a yellow light. 'Fast!' The Bianchi sped away and anyone who saw it pass saw a spark and heard the roar of the manchild. Pietro stamped on the pedals, wheezing with the effort. Fernando pulled down his beret and placed both hands on top of the concierge's, crushing them, and now he was spluttering, 'Slow down, slow down, slow down.' Pietro didn't slow down. The road to Piazzale Loreto led uphill. The boy rested his cheek against the handlebars, making himself lighter. Pietro stood up on the pedals and placed his chin atop Fernando's head for the final sprint, racing like he'd never raced before. 'We won,' he said when they arrived. 'We won, Fernando!' The Bianchi braked to a stop outside Anita's building.

'What did we win?'

Pietro pressed the intercom buzzer. 'I have a friend who lives here who wants to meet you.'

Fernando massaged his rear end as they entered, then pressed himself into Pietro's side.

'Don't be afraid.'

They inserted the Bianchi into the bike rack and climbed to Anita's floor. Her door was open. So was the door to the neighbouring flat, from which Silvia emerged. 'Good evening.' She had two braids and her usual lip gloss, hid her mobile in the pocket of her jeans, looked at Fernando. '*Ciao*.'

Fernando pressed his glasses back.

Silvia smiled at him. 'My name's Alice, what's yours?'

His face darkened.

'She's a friend of mine. Don't be shy.'

Silvia came closer, caressed his back. 'What's your name?'

The strange boy turned toward Pietro. 'My name is Fernando.' He laughed out of nowhere.

'That's a nice name.' Silvia gestured to the concierge and

took Fernando by the hand, leading him to the threshold of her flat. They were shy steps, and he held on to the handrail on the landing, undecided, then took confidence. Before entering he adjusted his beret, stared at Pietro one last time.

Pietro nodded.

And he went.

Through the window he could see him still, from behind, in the middle of the small sitting room, dwarfed by the loose-fitting duffel coat, by the shirt collar buttoned up tight against his throat. She helped him out of his coat, inviting him to sit down, and he discovered that his Alice was a kind young woman.

'He's sweet.' Anita's voice came through a tiny window in her pantry, from where she had observed the scene. She moved to open her front door and called Pietro inside. 'I didn't expect him to be so . . .'

Pietro went in.

'So defenceless.' Anita screwed up her curious eyes. 'Now tell me about the seaside with your son.'

Pietro took her promptly into his arms, embracing her completely, holding his Anita tight and kissing her hair, her cheeks, her forehead. Rubbed himself against her and she encouraged him, telling him the sea had been good for him.

He kept on without speaking, awkwardly, with his rigid arms and rough fingers that had never learned to caress, that fumbled, that had never learned to feel.

'You told your son. You told him.'

His hands felt Anita's soft skin, felt what can go missing in a lifetime. He tore them away, just for a moment, to bring out the jar from the backpack. The little something that Anita had asked of him.

She unscrewed the lid on the jar. 'Land of mine.' The sand was once more icy cold. She stuck two fingers in, stuck them in up to her knuckles, and Pietro did the same. Their land warmed up.

They sought each other in the sand.

'Please give him the letter, please please.'

They held each other in the sand.

Celeste rose to the surface of the sea and floated there. Pietro placed one hand beneath her back and another in her hair. The waves pulled her away. He held on to her and said, 'Don't get married.'

'I leave tomorrow.'

He squeezed her neck. 'Don't get married, I'm free now.' He found a hairpin in her hair and slipped it out. Then the waves wrested the witch away from him, dragged her toward the open sea where he could not swim.

'I'm free now.'

Pietro swam toward her even so, floundered and sank below the water, kicked and returned to the surface to draw breath, sought her with eyes burning from the salt. She was no longer to be seen. There was only the sea, and the blinding glare from the lighthouse. Then he saw her swimming towards the shore, getting out of the water, a shadow on the rocks.

Pietro opened his hand. All that remained of her was a copper hairpin and three broken hairs.

*

Fernando emerged from the flat along with his Alice, a button on his white shirt undone. Pietro waited for him on the landing. Silvia nodded to the concierge and stroked the strange boy's neck, pinched him on the cheek and went back inside. He told her she was his sweetheart. Fernando was red in the face and bewildered.

Pietro took his hand and felt that it was sweaty. Massaged his broad shoulders, zipped his duffel coat all the way up and tied his scarf the way Paola did. Led him down into the courtyard. They leaned on each other as they walked to the bike rack. Fernando continued to stare vacantly into space. The concierge lifted out the Bianchi and raised his eyes to the balconies above. Silvia's window was already dark. Anita appeared behind hers, her hair down and a hand pressed to the window. Pietro waited until he was at the front gate, and then for the first time blew her a kiss.

He loaded Fernando onto the top bar, steadying him with an arm when he leant to one side or the other. The Bianchi set off slowly and continued slowly for the entire trip. There was no need to pedal. It took them home and when they arrived the boy was almost asleep, bent over the handlebars and with his legs perched on the frame below. Pietro left the Bianchi outside the lodge. 'Your mother is waiting for you.'

Fernando got down and didn't move from the spot. Planted his feet and stared with eyes dark with sleep, undid his coat and scarf. Entered the lodge and waited in front of the concierge's flat, a dog scratching at the door.

'It's late, let's go up to your mother's.' Pietro opened his door. The boy entered first. Stopped at the kitchen table, took two steps toward the bed, entered the bedroom. Turned on the lamp and aimed it at the suitcase. 'My jewel.' Bowed his head and took off his beret, laid it on top of the biggest box, which held a rusty hairpin and the outfit of a young priest.

'Take care of your mother, Fernando.'

The boy's forehead furrowed. He pulled him to him, planting the concierge's cheek on his shoulder while his bare head flushed.

'Take care of your mother.' Pietro squeezed back. Led him out of the bedroom, washed his face. Then they climbed the stairs together, clinging to one another. He knocked.

Paola opened immediately. 'Where is your papa's hat?'

'We lost it.' Pietro laid a hand on her shoulder. 'It's my fault. I'm sorry.'

Fernando did not separate himself from the concierge.

She chewed her lip, bit down hard then kissed her son on the head. 'No Buraco for me. That lout Poppi was nowhere to be found.' She ushered her son inside. 'Goodnight, Pietro.'

'Goodnight.'

Fernando called to the concierge as his mother closed the door, called out the concierge's name when his mother tried to put him to bed beside her.

Pietro stared at their door, the peephole drilling a perfect bullseye. Then approached the lawyer's door and did not hear the television. Rang and rang again. Returned to his flat to collect his copy of the keys. Went back up the stairs and rang one last time. Then opened the door.

And he saw him, hanging from the ceiling, his face blue

and his feet grazing the floor. His mouth slightly open. An envelope protruded from a pocket of his dressing gown. On the floor was a card with the handwritten message, 'Mazel tov'.

# 43

The noose had cut into his neck, wreathing it with dried blood. The dressing gown was closed and the sheen of the silk reflected the gleam of a candle. Pietro went closer. The chair had overturned beside the card with the crest of the Grand Hotel and the words 'Reserved for Deluxe Vans'. Below that, in graceful handwriting, 'Mazel tov'. The wish for the ones left behind.

The lawyer's body spun on its own axis. The rope had been tied to a ceiling beam and it groaned with the weight. Poppi's eyes bulged, his nostrils were collapsing, his tongue stuck out. From his legs rose a sickly sweet stench. His shoulders sloped and his arms came forward as if they were clutching something. From his sleeves emerged manicured nails. Pietro stopped the body from spinning, noticed the can of tuna open on the table, an upright fork sticking out. Peered around, saw no sign of the cat. Saw the gramophone in front of the window, and the cycad, its curving leaves grazing the wall with the tribal masks. Took one down by the eye holes and turned back to Poppi. Closed the lawyer's eyes and settled the mask over his face, adjusting the elastic band at the back of his neck. *Forgive him his sins, O Lord.* Took the envelope from the pocket of the dressing gown, saw *Pietro* written in block letters. Opened it.

*I've gone to join my Daniele. Look for your love, I've ex-*

*plained to you where to find her. Talk to Celeste, tell her about Luca. Your son.*

*I knew. But as I told you, forgetfulness is what separates me from the gossips.*

The lawyer's body began to turn again.

*I still have time for a story that comes from your part of the country. There was a man, things for this man were going so-so, the Flood came and he was on the roof of his house so he wouldn't drown, he asks God with all his faith to be saved and in his heart he knows that God will save him.*

*A boat comes, the man refuses it because he's certain that the Lord will come to save him, so he says, No, thank you. Meanwhile the water is rising, another boat comes but he's waiting for God. Meanwhile the water has reached his throat, a third boat passes, No, thanks. So then he drowns.*

*When he arrives in Heaven and finally sees the Lord, he says to him, You promised to save me! God looks at him, says, Hold on now, I sent you three boats, what else do you want from me?*

*You've let two boats go by, Pietro – get on board the third one. Tell Luca who his father is. Don't leave this secret to Heaven as well.*

*One more thing: Thank you. If I've found the strength to become a first-class chandelier, I owe it to your sea. I've been a lonely man, less so when I met you. Gratitude is not of this world but of the other. And I already feel like I'm there.*

*Mazel tov, my friend. I'll look forward to seeing you again.*

# 44

Pietro waited for dawn with the lawyer. The glow crept up the walls and showed them one beside the other. His vigil continued. He removed the mask and thanked him. *Gratitude is of this world as well.* Took one of the lawyer's cold, hanging hands into his own, interlaced their fingers. Then walked away. Left the flat and headed for his own, arriving in the bedroom. The lamp had remained on and directed at the closed boxes. He knelt before the pieces of his memory. *I've never lost you, Celeste.* Said the same to the rosary at his wrist, *I've never lost you.*

Mist arrived with that prayer and covered Milan. Pietro stood, retrieved a plastic bag from the wardrobe and bent down over the boxes. Opened them and took the bell and the hairpin, the foil wrappers. Took the crucifix, the photographs, the chewing gum and all the rest. Took Fernando's hat and the elephant. Removed the lid from the largest box, picked up the young priest's gown. The black was still black, the cotton fabric ragged. He pulled out the rice-paper envelope with the Emilio Salgari postage stamp. Put everything into the bag and went to the kitchen. Tore up the lawyer's farewell card and tossed it in. Returned the keys to Poppi's flat to their hook and retrieved the post that had come for Luca. As he emerged from the building with the Bianchi he heard someone calling him, *Marcello, Marcello.*

He raised his head. Alice had just arrived at the cafe. Now

she came towards him. 'I wanted to invite you . . .' She looked at the bag hanging from one of the Bianchi's brake handles. 'Tonight there's a little going-away party for me at the cafe.'

'You're leaving?'

'I'm going back to Sardinia. You're all invited, you, the doctor and Fernando, his mother, everyone' – she looked up at the condominium – 'even the lawyer, who gave me his Siamese without telling me the cat had an attitude.'

Pietro smiled at her. 'Till tonight, then.' He patted her gently on the cheek and left. The cobbles made the jewels bounce in the bag. He hunched down over the top bar and let the Bianchi run. The mist obscured the streets. The concierge laboured to arrive at his destination, the black-and-white-striped wall of the cemetery. He left the bicycle beside the hut of a flower-seller and passed through the front gate. Left the gravel path as Poppi had explained, entered the underground passage between the wall tombs. As the sunlight stole up the walls it seemed to swallow up the tombs. From the far end he counted back seven panels. On the eighth was written *Celeste* in iron. Above it the witch smiled, a faraway look in her eyes, her face ravaged by time. Her husband was in the next photograph along, underground for the past five years. Pietro knelt down for the second time that day. *Ciao*, he said to her, and dug. Dug below the gravel. *Luca looks like me*. Dug as deep a hole as he could manage. *Our son looks like us*. Scraped and his nails blackened. Collapsed forward, bent but not praying. *I can't tell him I'm his father*, he brought his hands together, *but I promise you I'll protect him*. Sat up, grasped the bag and opened it, filled the hole with the pieces of his memory, one by one. *I promise you that I will protect him.* Last into the hole were Fernando's beret and the elephant. He covered them with earth and with the stones. What was left was the rice-paper envelope.

He tore it. Tore it again and again until he could no longer hold on to the shreds of the letter and of the photograph. They fell and scattered. Only then did he know himself to be divested of all that he had been.

Pietro leaned the Bianchi against the pole of the traffic light and buzzed the intercom of the studio flat. No one answered. Through the window he could see a lit wall. 'It's Pietro.' He held on to the window bars and tapped on the glass. 'It's me.'

The building door clicked open shortly after. Pietro entered and proceeded to the mezzanine floor.

'I was expecting Viola and him.' Luca stood in the doorway. He went back inside and climbed up into the loft with his shirt hanging out of his trousers, stretched out on the bed.

Pietro climbed to the loft. 'They're coming at nine-thirty.'

Luca held up his mobile, its screen dark. 'At nine-thirty they won't find me.' Raised his head from the pillow. 'The dolphins. I'm taking Sara on that dinghy.'

An overturned lamp lay on the floor beside the night table. Pietro set it right side up. 'When are you leaving?'

'I'm headed to the nursery school soon. Sara loves surprises.' He turned over on his side. 'First I have to do something.'

The lamp threw their shadows on the ceiling. Luca sat up against the headboard. His shadow narrowed and pierced Pietro's. 'Why have you done all this?'

'All this?'

'Lorenzo. The visit to the professor. Returning to Rimini. Coming here.' Luca stretched an arm into the empty half of the double bed. A tiny pair of pink pyjamas sat balled up on the second pillow. He gathered them up, folded them carefully, first the bottoms, then the top, and held tight that bundle that fitted into his two palms. 'Why have you?'

Pietro looked at him. His son's matted hair had been swept up into a horn at the centre of his head. His eyes were two bottomless pits. Pietro bent over and grasped him under the arms, tried to pull him to his feet. Luca wrapped his arms around Pietro's neck, thrust himself up and his legs slipped on the sheet. They didn't let go until they found themselves standing one before the other. They held on.

Then Luca changed his shirt, smoothed down the hair on his head. Climbed down from the loft and disappeared into the bathroom. Pietro sat down on the bed and placed the post on the bedside table. Stroked Sara's tiny, tiny pink pyjamas.

Luca came out of the bathroom and called up that he was ready.

Pietro stood and saw him put the old man's recorder into his leather bag.

# 45

Celeste passed the rocks and continued on her way.

Pietro held on to the hairpin and three broken hairs. *Damn you, God.* The sea pushed him down. He flailed, sank below the water. The current dashed him against the sea floor. *You've never given me anything.* He sunk into the sand. Awaited the end with open arms. The current suddenly drew him up, forced him to draw a breath. *Damn you.*

He flailed again and reached the rocks, climbed up. His feet were stones bound to his ankles. He put on his trousers only, limped down the jetty, down the promenade, raised his eyes to the Grand Hotel and reached the fountain of the four horses. Continued on to the witch's house, walked around it. Her window was dark. He picked up a handful of gravel, threw and threw again until the light went on. The shadow of the witch stretched out along the wall. 'Celeste,' he shouted. 'Celeste.'

The window opened. Pietro saw only a hand holding a scrap of paper, letting it drop. It was their punishment.

# 46

Father and son left the studio flat. Pietro followed Luca onto the street. He went through the street door last and pulled it shut without locking it. 'Have a good trip.'

Luca hesitated on the pavement, was blurred by the mist. Came closer to the concierge.

Pietro raised his arms but not before his son did the same. Luca embraced him, enveloped him, pulled him close. Then walked away alone. Before he turned the corner he looked back, seeking him one last time, but he was no longer there.

Pietro had gone back into the courtyard to wait.

Viola arrived an hour later. Pietro heard her voice through the street door. 'I called him last night and he confirmed nine-thirty.'

He heard Riccardo as well. 'Buzz again.'

'He's not here.'

'I'll call him now.' Riccardo cleared his throat. 'His phone's off.'

Pietro came out onto the street. Viola stood before him. 'You?'

'I brought the doctor his post.'

'Did you see him?'

'He's gone back to Rimini.'

Riccardo was leaning against the SUV. He swung his crutches their way and hobbled over. 'What did you say?'

'He's gone back to Rimini.'

Viola looked at Riccardo. 'Let's let him be. Please.'

'He said he'd stay there for a few days,' said the concierge.

'A few days,' she sighed.

'With the little girl,' Pietro added.

Riccardo shook one of his crutches and spun around. 'I'm going to Rimini too.'

'Wait, we can . . .' Viola fiddled with a button on her coat.

'I'm tired of waiting.' Riccardo hurried toward the car. 'Do you feel like driving?'

Viola leaned against the pole of the traffic light, along with the Bianchi. She recognized it and stared. Pulled a brake lever. The concierge stared at her and his bicycle. The red suited it. He saw again the witch on the top bar and the young priest who carried her into the night by the sea. Pietro closed his eyes. 'I'll go with you.'

# 47

The old man was waiting at the entrance to the house of the pomegranate trees.

The doctor nodded and made his way into the kitchen, laid his coat and leather bag on a chair. He had not yet looked at the man. Did so now. He was a skeleton in his nicest outfit.

'Go right ahead, my Andrea is through there.' The old man accompanied him down the hallway and returned to the kitchen alone. Closed a packet of biscuits with a clothes peg and lowered the rolling shutter, reassembled the stovetop percolator from the pieces in the dish rack. Returned it to a cupboard and started to fold tea cloths but stopped because Luca had returned.

'You've seen how handsome my Andrea is? More handsome than when he was alive.'

Luca sat down and wedged the bag between his feet. From it he drew out what was needed. Poured the tranquillizers into a glass that he found on the table, inserted the stethoscope's earpieces into his ears. Returned the recorder.

Beyond the window the mist had turned to fog.

The old man left the kitchen and walked down the hallway to his son's room. Luca unwrapped the syringe and filled it. *Ankle, ball, ankle*. And he went.

Pietro kept an eye out as he drove ever since they had entered the motorway. The steering wheel was crumbling inside. He held it where the leather was ragged, stuck two fingers in, withdrew them to change gears.

'Would you mind going faster?' Riccardo was behind him, his leg in the cast stretched across the rear seats. Viola twisted a lock of hair in the seat beside Pietro, slowly knocked her knees together, gazed out at the descending fog.

'Would you mind going faster?'

Pietro stiffened his fingers into the seams and the leather covering the steering wheel gave slightly. He did not accelerate. Riccardo said something to him. Pietro stared at the point of the windscreen where the fog split.

'Everything OK?' Viola asked.

Pietro nodded and accelerated.

Luca took seven steps down the hallway, entered Andrea's room. The old man had removed the bed's sidewalls and now sat next to his son, supporting his head. 'Last night we watched the 1982 World Cup final, then I pulled out the tube.' He brushed aside the hair from his forehead. In front of them the whiteboard held a pristine piece of Bristol board. The television was off. So, too, were the machines. They could hear the trains rolling by beyond the wall of fog.

'My Andrea was happy when I told him that the doctor had agreed, that we wouldn't be separated for long.' He coughed. 'We'd made a pact, he and I: together. That we'd leave this place together. I had the courage for him. I don't have it for myself.'

Luca went closer and saw that the Bristol at the board

wasn't entirely white. Two black strips marked the top right corner and a band of blue ran along the bottom.

'Please have a seat, Doctor.' The old man pushed the armchair in his direction with one foot, without leaving his son. 'Sit down, please.'

Luca did not sit. Instead he approached the bed with the glass.

The old man covered his son's eyelids. 'Andrea asked me to do it.' He straightened up and took the glass, looked inside. 'He asked me to do it with his eyes.' He drank. Rolled up a sleeve of his shirt, revealing a bare, reed-like arm. Offered it up to him.

Pietro pulled his fingers from the seams of the steering wheel, turned and moved into the left lane. Accelerated again and returned to the centre lane. He raised his eyes to the rear-view mirror.

Riccardo was staring at him. 'Did he tell you why he's going back to Rimini, Pietro?' Without waiting for an answer he said to Viola, 'Hand me the documents in the glove box, would you?' He left off speaking, looking as they all were at a pool of water that came out of the fog and shone on the asphalt ahead of them. The pool came closer and they understood what it was in the instant it hit them. Water and rotten leaves. It broke open and a clump of leaves landed on the windscreen, on the back window, covered the side windows. The concierge turned on the windscreen wipers. The leaves lifted while Riccardo took from Viola the folder with the car's documents.

A leaf got stuck in the corner of the windscreen. Pietro turned off the wipers just in time to save it. He scrutinized the veins, some still with traces of green. The leaf stalk was broken. The wind threatened to carry the leaf away. The concierge moved into the right lane. From behind the hand of Riccardo reached forward, holding a Polaroid. He turned it round. It was the same ultrasound stuck up on the Martinis' fridge.

The leaf held out, then the wind took it away. Pietro heard the voice: 'It's Sara. It's my daughter.'

'He's my son.' The old man held his naked arm in the air and caressed his Andrea. Carefully shifted his limbs as he had learned to over the years, first the legs, then the shoulders and finally the head with a hand behind his neck, slowly. Lay down beside him and took his hand into his own. 'We're Rossi and Altobelli, world champions.' Then the doctor nodded. The old man settled his head onto the single pillow and now Luca could see them together, the father's face frightened, the son's at peace.

A thread of voice remained to the old man. 'Your father looks like you.' He still had his arm up in the air. 'Mr Pietro looks like you. You must be proud of your father.'

Riccardo held up Sara's ultrasound. Viola took it from him and said, 'Stop it, please.'

Pietro moved to the middle lane and slowed down. He turned over his hands. Now he controlled the wheel with the backs of his hands and looked at his palms. They were those of a child, smooth. His right hand curled into a cup. He closed it slightly and the hollow became deeper, like in the night by the sea, under the window, after the witch had dropped the scrap of paper with their punishment. He had picked it up and laid it on that palm, gazed on it from different angles. On it was written: *Forget*. The punishment was absence. He had raised his head to the window, now closed again. *Celeste*, he had called to her, *Celeste*. The witch's silhouette was visible through the curtains, *Celeste*. It was the last time the young priest saw her. Witches fly away. Pietro gripped the steering wheel again.

'She's my daughter,' said Riccardo. 'My child.'

The concierge clenched his right hand. 'Does anyone else know?'

The rain had started again.

'Does anyone else know?' Pietro repeated.

'The three of us,' said Riccardo. 'It's weighed on us for two years now.'

Viola covered her eyes with her hand and leaned her elbow against the window, crying. The concierge took her other hand and closed it in his own.

The SUV was approaching the bridge over the River Po.

# 48

Pietro maintained his speed. An estate car moved in front of them and he passed it. He let go of Viola's hand and grasped the steering wheel. Passed another car and accelerated toward the bridge.

In the house of the pomegranate trees Luca held up the old man's arm. He massaged it where there was still a bit of flesh. 'Mr Pietro looks like you.' The old man's voice was a death rattle. 'You must be proud of your father.'

Luca massaged the arm for the last time, a caress, then said, 'My father died five years ago.'

Ahead the lights of the barriers indicated the location of the broken guard rail. Pietro slowed down and the SUV started across the bridge. At the same moment Luca removed the cap from the syringe and the old man took hold of his own trembling arm. 'God bless you, Doctor.' Luca pierced the skin and as he lowered the plunger he stared at the tired father.

Pietro stared at Viola collapsed against the car window. The SUV moved to the left lane. The lights of the barriers came through the fog. There began the bank of the river and there Pietro turned the wheel. The SUV struck the temporary rail and broke through.

The old man died gazing at his son. Pietro with the words of Celeste. *The past is in this letter, a past thirty years long. Yes, it's me, and I'm about to die. I don't want to take the biggest secret with me.*

*His name is Luca. He's our son.*

*That night in the sea, Pietro. That night a witch once again became a mother and chose silence. That's how I tried to protect you. The truth is that I was only protecting myself. Forgive me.*

*Luca is the future we never had, but he is us. He lives with his wife, Viola, and their little girl, on the second floor of a condominium that's looking for a new concierge. If you want, you could be that concierge. And this is the last thing I leave to chance in my life.*

*Call the person whose name I'll write at the end of this letter. He's a friend and the condominium administrator. I asked him to send you this letter. Take care of Luca. Watch over our son. He's a boy on the ball.*

*Pietro, I've never stopped feeling like you were with me. Never. I wanted to tell you with this flesh while it lasts. It's an honest love, and I'll take it with me where I go. And wherever I am, witch or ballerina, I'll be ready. First with the heel, then with the toe.*

## *Author's Note*

All references to real facts and persons are purely coincidental. For narrative reasons, slight modifications have been made to the topography of Milan and Rimini. The song quoted in chapter 36 is 'Il mare d'inverno' (The sea in winter) by Loredana Bertè.